In a crime-filled town run by thieves and gangsters, one man stands against the darkness. Jack Breeder possesses an inexplicable talent for finding things, even when someone doesn't want them found. After ruining several high-value schemes, a dark underground syndicate decides Jack needs a career change.

When a mysterious job, too good to resist, turns from a simple retrieval to a high stakes game of lost and found, Jack finds himself racing against the clock to save the people he loves.

The Finder tells the tale of how far one man will go to save his way of life.

I0549543

The Finder
By Steven Rome

The Finder

By Steven Rome

Published by FrostFire Publishing

Copyright 2013 Steven Rome

CHAPTER ONE

It was cold. A strange, hollow type of cold permeated the air, surrounding Jack in a way he had never felt before. He sat on the edge of the metal bed; at least what passed for a bed - in reality it was nothing more than a thick metal shelf that connected to the wall and the floor. Everything was fuzzy; he couldn't remember how he had gotten to this strange cold place...

Jack Breeder was someone who possessed skills that didn't really fit in with society's idea of normal. He was good at finding things, good at solving puzzles and quite good at drinking whiskey. But he wasn't particularly good at much else. He was never able to hold a steady girlfriend, or even commit to a monthly magazine subscription.

No, everything needed to be fluid, changeable, new and fresh. That forced Jack into becoming a *finder*, someone people called upon when something went missing--by accident or on purpose. It wasn't the prettiest job, and the benefits were lousy, but the pay was good, the scenery always changed, and so did the people. Not that everyone was a huge Breeder fan. He had made just as many enemies as friends, but that didn't bother him much and when it did, Jack Daniels was a reliable cure.

Last night, Jack had received one of the strangest job offers he had ever laid eyes on. The thunderstorms outside his rural home had been in high gear; the trees surrounding his century-old log cabin were big and sturdy, but they still made a lot of ruckus in a big storm.

Just after midnight, a young messenger delivered a letter with no return address. Jack had invited the guy in, to weather the storm, but the message-bearer would have no part of it. He shoved the letter in Jack's hand and took off running. Something had spooked the guy badly; Jack didn't know what it was, but it was clear the cowardly carrier wanted rid of that letter--and fast.

The fire crackled next to the old bearskin rug, half hidden under the giant tattered lounge chairs where Jack conducted all of his business. Jack always preferred to think of himself as someone who performed favors for those who needed it, and the money was just a benefit on the side. The letter reeked of a strong noxious smell, like something pulled from a putrid swamp, or the carcass of an animal that had been dead for a few weeks. Holding the letter out as far away from him as he could while still being able to read it, the letter began...

"Dear Jack,

Some associates of mine informed me that you are quite good at retrieving the un-retrievable. They say you were instrumental in bringing back their precious African artifact to the Lemante estate. Outstanding job, old boy, no one ever thought those devils would be devious enough to hide it in an ancient cave like that!

If you truly are as good as they say you are, then I may have a job for you. My granddaughter and I had a wonderful time on vacation, until we were on our way home. At the airport, someone bumped into her, seemingly quite randomly, and then disappeared. By the time she realized that her favorite pendant was gone, so was the gentleman. But this isn't a case of petty theft; the pendant was actually a gift I had given her as a child, purchased long ago on one of our adventures in Tahiti.

While on business there, I came in contact with a quite exotic wares dealer. He had many things in his shop, from shrunken heads and strangely colored feathers to jewelry and big, big knives. He said the jewels were taken from a local idol called Odalos Ne. He went on to say that the idol was sacred, and he had taken extreme risk by even considering selling such a thing.

Of course, when my granddaughter took a shine to it, I procured it right then and there.

This was the only piece of jewelry ever made from those stones. I must have it back! If you're as good as I've heard, find the pendant and return it to me for your reward. Enclosed you will find a picture, a business card and a small stipend to secure your services.

Godspeed."

Jack was perplexed. He continued sipping his fine, aged whiskey from a cracked glass with two ice cubes--any more took up precious space. It was smooth, like drinking liquid gold laced with heaven. He looked down; lying on the ground was a small picture of a pendant obscuring a business card with only the name "Jim Tanner" visible.

Jack bent down and picked up the goods, examining the picture. The pendant was a beautiful gold piece, oval with jewel encrusted loops on all sides. In the middle of the oval sat a beautiful, large red stone. It was mesmerizing. The gem looked like crystallized fire. The business card bore Jim's full name and address, with only the title "Importer Exporter." Jack knew that these guys were usually well-connected with the underground and places that dealt in backwater goods.

"So, why couldn't this guy just find the pendant on his own, with those types of connections?" Jack wondered out loud to himself.

A shimmer of light caught the corner of his eye and attention. The sparkling fire glimmered off the crystal that fell out of the envelope. It was the clearest diamond he had ever seen, smooth on all sides, and as pristine as they came. He knew how much the gem must be worth, and consequently just how serious Mr. Tanner must be.

Jack set out the very next morning to talk to his contacts in the slum district. If anyone knew where to start looking for such an item, it would be them.

CHAPTER TWO

Rusty and Caleb McEntyre were shady types, all right. Since the day they were born, they had known nothing but stealing food and finding places for shelter, but they had done well for themselves after decades on the streets. One or the other, Jack never could tell which, was heading up the local thieves' guild; if someone stole something in this town, those two knew about it.

"Rusty," Jack greeted a small, portly figure, leaning down over a wooden desk inspecting a tall pile of coins.

"Jack, you troublemaker, what brings you down to the better end of town?" the man asked.

Rusty fully believed those who had to do without were simply better people than those who had money. He knew Jack had money, but Rusty also knew he was more than willing to spend it on a good time at the local pub, and that made him one of them. Rich people didn't associate with those who would frequent a pub, he rationalized.

Jack explained the situation to Rusty. He told him all about the letter, the gem, the strange messenger, and the Odalos Ne pendant.

The thieves' guild was like a union for the shady characters in town. No one was allowed to steal anything without running it by the head of the guild, and giving over a small percentage of the take. With eyes and ears everywhere, the guild knew everything worth knowing.

Through blackmail and organizing together, they had become quite influential. They didn't have the firepower of a gang, or the resources of the mob, but those things weren't necessary. As long as they stuck to the shadows and ran things on the down low, the bigger fish ignored their existence.

Jack could tell Rusty definitely knew something. The averted eyes and sudden perspiration on Rusty's brow gave that away; but he wasn't exactly forthcoming with information.

Jack stood silently, his arms crossed. His left foot tapped the ground impatiently.

"Alright, since it's you, I'll tell you what I know, but you didn't hear it from me. One of my guys got an offer for $50,000 if they could get their hands on that pendant. Some guy from the east side gave him all the information he needed, from the exact moment Tanner would be coming through the airport with his granddaughter to the kind of clasp on the chain," Rusty confessed. "All he had to do after the fact was drop it off in the broken building on 33rd and pick up his money," he continued, extremely gratified. "Of course, I said for 25% of the cut he was more than welcome to make the grab."

Jack rolled his eyes.

"What? It's good business," boasted Rusty.

Jack laughed it off and thanked him for the information. He couldn't have asked for a better lead, and besides, as long as Rusty kept misplacing things, people would need Jack to go find them.

The building on 33rd Street had been condemned for years. Down a back alley, between an old industrial park and a water treatment plant, it was an ideal location for something that needed no witnesses.

Jack felt the unwelcoming steely stare of someone watching him as his old Jeep pulled up outside the building. Someone didn't want him to be there. Jack had been in cloak-and-dagger type situations a million times before, but he always felt nervous when his cover might have been blown. There was no other sensation in the world like the gut-twisting feeling he got when he was someplace he wasn't supposed to be, and someone else knew he was there.

He pushed open the half-broken door; all that kept it from falling apart was the boards on either side of it. The cracking of the ancient wooden fibers didn't allow for a silent entry. Jack poked around the old factory floor, where they used to make bakery goods until the company went under several years ago. He could taste stale flour in the air. Most of the machinery was still intact, but in need of serious repair. His focus drifted, wondering why someone hadn't bought the plant and started it back up again, since the previous owners had left everything behind.

His thoughts of fresh baked goods were cut short by that feeling again; someone was staring at the back of his head, right into his soul. The floorboards creaked, the sound coming from only a few machines over. It wasn't paranoia, someone was following him.

Jack darted through the old swinging doors directly beside him into the next room. He ducked down behind an old desk and waited for his pursuers to give the chase. The room had no windows and only one entrance. The bare green walls were dirty and covered with cobwebs. An ancient computer sat, broken into pieces, beside the desk. Jack figured if he was being followed, the choke point would at least give him a tactical advantage to fight back from. Minutes went by without any further sign of anyone following. Nothing moved. Nothing made a sound, beside his own heartbeat. He began to wonder if the noise might have been an animal after all.

He crept out from behind the desk and over to the door. No one could be seen outside, just a bunch of dust in the air; he must have stirred them up along the way, running around like a lunatic. Not that he had lived through as many close calls as he had without being smart in the face of danger. Sometimes smart meant running.

The swinging door creaked, just like all the other furniture in the rundown factory. Jack was finding the age of the building made slinking around stealthily exceedingly difficult. As he walked further into the facility, it felt as if the air itself were being sucked out of the building. The air was cold, but not in the normal sense of cold. It was the kind of cold he only felt in the presence of something sinister.

Jack had just begun rounding the corner of the next hallway when he paused to look to the room on his left. A solid steel door, with riveted markings on both sides, stuck out among an otherwise door-less hallway. He tried the doorknob only to find it locked. Jack reached into his back pocket to pull out a small, black, zipped pouch, containing tools of the trade. He pulled out two shiny tools - one with a straight edge and the other a slight crick - before setting his sights on the lock.

The weird feeling of being watched pricked the back of his neck again. He stopped to look around. After reassuring himself the coast was clear, he resumed the delicate operation.

It only took Jack a few tries before he heard the rewarding click of the lock accepting his request to open. He turned the knob with caution and pushed on the door. As the door squeaked open, Jack reached behind his head with his left hand. A sharp pain in the back of his neck prompted him to feel around for a second before bringing his hand back in front of his face, only to see his fingers tinged red.

He dropped to his knees, paused and then continued to the floor. With his eyes half open, he saw a pair of large black shoes and finely-tailored, silver cuffed pants standing in front of him before everything went dark.

CHAPTER THREE

Stumbling to his feet, Jack shook his head back and forth violently, trying to shake the sense back into his fuzzy head. He felt the back of his head with his left hand to find there was a bandage over the wound. He glanced around the room, looking for his assailant, only to find nothing but the metal shelf that had served as his bed, and a small desk. The room was windowless, the walls bare. The only noticeable difference between that room and the rest of the building was a lack of dust or dirt. The scent of bleach hung in the air. Upon further inspection, Jack realized someone had not only cleaned the room, but they had removed all traces of the blood from the blow to his head.

As he approached the desk, he felt the strange sense again, the same one he had felt the night before; as if someone or something was watching him.

The small blue metal desk had only one drawer, already cracked halfway open. He reached for it and with a gentle pull, the drawer flopped out of the desk, spilling its contents to the ground.

There, lying on the floor in the middle the drawer, was the Odalos Ne pendant, with a small piece of yellow paper. Jack reached down, picking up the jewelry in his left hand and paper in the right.

He examined the necklace. It was flawless. The pictures failed to capture how mesmerizing it was. After staring at the shining gems in fascination for a moment, Jack glanced over at the paper. Scribbled on one side was a short, yet poignant message.

Here is your precious pendant. We suggest you stop looking for things that don't belong to you. Next time, don't expect a bandage.

He wasn't sure what to make of the message or why the pendant had appeared out of the air, but he wasn't about to look a gift horse in the mouth. Taking a moment to tuck the items in his jacket pockets, Jack made his way toward the front door as quickly as he could. He wanted to return the pendant and be done with the case. Fighting bad guys to retrieve artifacts was one thing, but being stalked, attacked and given triage by his assailant was too weird, even for him.

When Jack arrived back to tell Rusty the good news, he was nowhere to be found. The shop was empty. Jack thought it was strange, but they were crafty fellows, and he never could tell what they were up to.

He retrieved Jim Tanner's business card from the pocket of his leather jacket. The drive wouldn't be far and he still had pictures to show off, once the necklace was returned to its rightful owners. He decided to skip bragging to Rusty and return the pendant right away, rather than wait around worrying about someone who probably didn't want to be found, anyway.

Jack and his good old black army Jeep pulled up in front of the address marked on the business card. The roads leading there were more like dirt paths without trees; there were no signs or houses, only one winding road that stopped right there. He understood in an instant that the address was no ordinary place. There was no house. A large tree stump, twice the size of his Jeep, was the only thing waiting for him. In the center of the stump was a purple handkerchief, wrapped around a large rock. Tucked in the package was a small card identical to the one Jack held with Tanner's information on one side. He flipped it over.

"You have been warned" was written in bold red lettering on the back of the card.

Jack realized it had never been about the pendant. He now knew why the messenger had been so spooked, and why Rusty's guy had been given such specific information. The whole thing was a set up from the very beginning.

His days of finding stolen goods, thwarting painstakingly made plots and generally shining light in the darkest corners of town were catching up with him. He had made a lot of enemies in the underground. Figuring out which one was behind the theft of the pendant wasn't going to be easy.

Someone had gone to a lot of trouble to give him a very strong, non-lethal message. He wondered why anyone would go to such trouble just to run him off, when murder was the easier alternative. With such an elaborate set up, they could have easily killed him and no one would've ever known who had done it.

Someone very powerful was advising Jack to consider a career change.

CHAPTER FOUR

The loud crack of Rusty's stool hitting the ground echoed throughout the pub. Rusty's feet didn't reach the floor when he sat on one of those things, which was why he preferred to sit in a booth. The tall man standing by the bar had said something rather offensive to provoke Rusty into jumping down off his stool. Jack walked into the establishment just in time to see the animated pair headed for a blowup.

Rusty was a short and stout fellow, with a reddish brown beard halfway down his body and hair color to match. Most people would never expect to hear the kind of loud and sarcastic language he loved to use from someone who looked like a gnomish teddy bear. Even still, Rusty had a pretty even temperament. He much preferred winning a battle of wits to throwing punches. Rusty could talk circles around the biggest lawyers in town, out talk the slickest politicians without a second thought or even con a grandmother right out of her dentures.

In any other situation, Jack wouldn't have worried for a second. Rusty could talk his way out of being taken to hell by the devil himself. But this was different--the tall man in the black trench coat was wiry and jittery--something wasn't right. Jack recognized the body language of someone who was agitated out of their mind, on a foreign substance.

"Listen, son," Rusty said to the tall man. "Just remember who I am. I'm Rusty McEntyre, the best street man you'll ever run across. Now, sit back down. No one's afraid of someone who looks like they're selling silverware out of their trench coat."

The man laughed. "Like that means anything," he responded. "No one cares who you are and I'm not giving you any money. If you're so tough, come and get it."

Rusty sized up the tall man. "Why must they always do it the hard way?" he retorted out loud. "Hey, Simon," he yelled across the bar. "Come meet my friend, the spoon salesman, here." The tall man turned to see who he was yelling at, but when he turned his head, Rusty stomped on the man's foot. While hobbling on one leg, he didn't even notice Rusty had taken his silver money clip, counted a specific amount of money and slipped the rest back into the guy's pocket.

"You're dead, dwarf," the man yelled, pulling his arm back with a balled up fist. Rusty shut his eyes and braced himself for the blow.

"You do enjoy riling the natives," Jack remarked.

Rusty opened one eye. He looked up, squinting, to see Jack's hand around the tall man's fist. He chuckled deeply. The tall man swung around in the opposite direction, turning a full 360, whaling his foot toward Jack's head and breaking free of the hold. Jack ducked the kick and grabbed the man by his coat, in an especially quick move, sending the tall man sprawling to the floor.

"What can I say?" Rusty said with a shrug and a smile. "I'm a people person."

"Yeah, I can see that," Jack replied. "Maybe you should help your new friend up."

Rusty stood over the tall man's head. "I told you not to test my patience. I'm just glad I didn't have to hurt you," Rusty stretched out his arms, twisting them around, popping his knuckles. "Lucky for you, Jack interfered before I had to get physical."

Jack rolled his eyes. "Get up," he said, dragging the man back to his feet by his collar. "Get out of here, before Rusty gets physical." The man still seemed slightly confused by what had just happened, but scurried out the door.

"Thanks, Jack," he nodded.

"My pleasure," Jack quipped. "Now, how about you buy me a drink with the money you just took from him as thanks, and tell me where you've been. I've been looking for you for days."

"Uh, yeah. Sorry about that," Rusty answered sheepishly.

He turned to the bartender and ordered four shots of Jack Daniels for the booth in the corner, their usual place for going to talk things out. He explained to Jack how the situation with the pendant didn't feel right. The information given to his man was too accurate, almost like they wanted to steal their own pendant. No one knew that much information about something they didn't own, he insisted.

Jack spent the next few minutes retelling the story of the strange business offer to find the pendant in the first place. Of course, Rusty was more interested in the gem that came in the envelope than what had happened to Jack.

"So, was it a big gem?" Rusty asked, leaning over the table eagerly. "What color was it? What shape?"

Jack grimaced. "Focus, Rusty," he said with a sigh as he tossed back a shot. The warm infusion of alcohol refueled his tolerance.

"Right. Sorry. Go on, go on," Rusty said. He raised his hand, catching the bartender's eye and then pointed to a beer.

Jack continued the story of the strange cold place, the feeling of someone watching him, the medical care he received from his attacker, and the pendant being conveniently placed in plain sight.

"Someone was trying to send you a message, I take it," Rusty deduced, stroking his beard.

"I think that's an understatement," Jack answered. "Listen, old friend, I need to find your man on the street. I need to know who he got that information from and track down the people who were so kind as to warn me, after that exciting wild goose chase."

"You already did," said Rusty in a matter of fact kind of way.

"What?" Jack said with alarmed tone.

"You just kicked his butt," Rusty proclaimed

rather proudly. "That was Shane. My man from the east side. He didn't want to give me my cut from the job, even though I allowed him to do it in my town. Can you imagine the nerve?"

Jack put his hands on top of his head out of exasperation. "I need that guy to tell me what he knows," said Jack.

"I don't think he's going to want to take your call after that little incident," Rusty chuckled. "Not to worry." Rusty pulled out the money he had liberated from Shane's silver clip. "I have a feeling he's going to want this back," he added. "When Shane realizes it's gone, he'll stop by the shop to pick it up. One way or the other."

Jack reached into his pocket and pulled out a small clump of cash and then tossed it on the table in a hurry. He knew the only way he was going to find the people who set him up was by talking to the tall cloaked figure named Shane.

Rusty threw back his head, guzzling the last of his beer, as Jack's hand grabbed him by the sleeve, jerking him out of the booth. His mug fell back onto the table with a crash, breaking the beer holder into pieces. He waved to the annoyed bartender who was drying similar mugs behind the counter.

Rusty stopped at the door, turned back toward the bar and then raised his hand. "Actually, give me one for the road."

Jack's hand reached in through the doorway, grabbing Rusty by the collar and yanked him outside.

CHAPTER FIVE

Rusty spent most of the trip back to his shop fishing for information about the gem Jack received as payment for his fake job. Jack, on the other hand, wasn't the least bit interested in conversation. His mind was racing, trying to work out how to best handle the interrogation. Not that he was a stranger to interrogating uncooperative suspects.

His job often consisted of going from one strung-out, delusional, paranoid schizophrenic to the next, in the hope of finding a clue. Jack had become pretty good at learning when people were telling the truth. Most people were willing to talk, it was just a matter of knowing the right thing to say.

They wanted to talk. They wanted to tell him, sometimes bragging, about those kinds of things. The only thing stopping them from talking was fear. Some people feared retribution from whoever they were tattling on, while others were convinced Jack was working with the law.

Truth be told, Jack wasn't a big fan of the law either. Years ago, Jack's best friend, Davis, had been a sergeant at the 14th precinct. They had been the best of friends. Jack used his unusual ability to track down missing objects, and sometimes people, while his law enforcement ally kept the rest of the police department off his back. Not to mention the paperwork; Jack hated paperwork.

The partnership was a beautiful thing; Jack was unstoppable and the entire department was enamored with his ability to track down just about anything—he was even better than their best detectives. As time went on, the sergeant grew more and more popular. Jack was not one to take much credit, and even when he did, there was no way he would ever become an official policeman. Jack liked his freedom and enjoyed being a freelancer, so the credit naturally fell to Davis. Before long, the commissioner took note of the cold cases being solved at such a swift pace.

Next came the promotions. First to lieutenant, and then captain, and eventually chief of the 14th precinct. Davis became increasingly less grateful for the work Jack was doing to close each one of his precious cases.

Sometimes things went wrong. The art of finding things wasn't exactly black and white; sometimes suspects wouldn't talk, or didn't get the chance to, before meeting their untimely end. Sometimes it took longer to get the job done than someone sitting behind a desk doing paperwork would have liked. Sometimes trails went cold.

The pair, who were once inseparable, were under constant stress by the heavy weight of expectations. Jack became a tool of the department and, worse yet, a tool being used by his best friend. When Jack confronted Davis about the situation, he explained as best he could that a job like his required freedom. If he were going to continue to find things, to be the person everyone expected him to be, then Davis needed to loosen his grip and let Jack do what needed to be done.

The chief wasn't the least bit interested in his friend's strife. "We have hundreds of cases to solve and more come in every day," Davis said. "The commissioner will be retiring in a few years and these cases are going to get me that promotion. You need to get out there, Jack, and solve these cases. Cut corners, if you have to. I don't care. Just get it done."

Jack was astonished. He didn't find things for personal glory, let alone the glory of someone else. For him, it was about doing the one thing in life that he was good at. It was the one thing in life that he could do to make a difference for real people, and to earn an honest living.

"Who cares about promotion," retorted Jack. "We're helping people like Mr. Jones and Ms. Hermalas, and others who need our help."

"Wrong, Jack," snapped Davis. "This promotion means everything. Once I'm commissioner, things will be different. You'll have all the recognition you ever dreamed of. You'll be rich and I'll be powerful. In ten years, I'll run for mayor and, with the famous finder by my side, who knows how far my career will go. I mean, you'll be well paid, I'll make sure of that. Don't you worry."

Jack knew then and there that things had changed. It wasn't about helping people, for him, anymore. It was all about the damned promotion.

Jack was nothing more than a tool, being used in a political power grab.

"No," Jack said. "We're helping people right here, right now. If you get a promotion on the way, that's great, but I'm not interested in big money or fame. This is what I'm good at. How long have you known me? Twenty years, now? Have I ever cared about money? No. My payment is seeing the expression on someone's face when they finally receive the help they have been looking for. That should be your payment, too."

"Get off your high horse," Davis demanded. "You wouldn't be anywhere, without me. You know that. This was never about the stupid people. They're all ungrateful, anyway. Screw them. They're just the stepping stones on the road to our fame and fortune. You'll thank me, when you're calling me Mr. Mayor. No, Mr. Governor. Heck, why not Mr. President?" he laughed.

Jack stood from his chair, fists clenched and knuckles white. "You've lost your way," Jack said with brooding anger. "You don't care about anyone but yourself anymore. Do you?"

"Ha," mocked the chief, walking around the desk to place his hand on Jack's shoulder. "I care about what matters. And I'll be dragging you along with me, since you can't see the bigger picture. Face it, without me you would be off in some jungle somewhere, working for trinkets. Keep your mouth shut, your eyes on the prize and solve these cases as quickly as possible."

Jack smiled brightly at the man who used to be

his friend. They both slowly started laughing together. Jack nodded and laughed harder still. Davis was still laughing as Jack's knuckles collided with the side of his jaw. In a single, swift, right hook, Jack shattered the 20 year relationship, and three of his former friend's teeth.

Almost as quickly, a rookie who had seen Jack throw the punch alerted the rest of the precinct. It took about the same amount of time again for a number of them to crowd the office, take Jack to the ground and begin dishing out a round of immediate in-house "justice." After five of Jack's ribs were broken, his nose was bloodied and his jaw dislocated, the chief called off his dogs.

"Let him up," Davis ordered.

Jack was ushered to his feet, the taste of blood flooding his mouth. Wobbling and grimacing, Jack stood before the man who, not so long ago, he would've taken a bullet for.

"If I ever see you again, you're going to fall down five flights of stairs in a single-story building, more than once," threatened the chief. "Do we understand each other?"

Jack nodded, backing out of the crowd, clutching his arm to his injured side. When the emergency room doctors inquired how he had got his injuries, Jack simply responded, "I was keeping my eyes on the prize."

Rusty was still going on about the shiniest gems he had ever seen when the Jeep pulled up outside his place of business. Jack hadn't heard one word he said the entire trip; not that Rusty had noticed, he could listen to himself talk for hours. It was one of Jack's favorite things about Rusty--it made conversations easy. Rusty talked while Jack kept right on going.

There was no sign of Shane, or anyone else for that matter, at the old shop. The front door was deceptive in appearance, with a crude, old rusted padlock and chain. No one suspected a rundown shop was a master thief's headquarters. Rusty unlocked the door, still chattering on about the fabulous world of gems.

Jack pulled a flashlight from his inside pocket and investigated each room for any signs of someone being there recently. The beam of light stemming from his hand explored every crevice in the room. Nothing was to be found, except for a gang of dust bunnies and some insects that moved too quickly to be identified.

"Have you ever considered a maid?" Jack inquired out loud, looking behind a box that was hiding moving wall paper.

"Aye, I did," said Rusty. "Let's just say things didn't work out and now I have to stay 500 yards away from a house on the lower south side," he grumbled humorously, chuckling.

Jack shook his head. "There's only one way into this place, right?"

Rusty nodded in agreement, heading off to another room. Jack flipped on a light and maneuvered a couple of chairs to the wall opposite the door. With their backs against the wall, no one could sneak by. He turned off his light. It would be dusk soon and he had a feeling that would be when Shane would show up. Rusty reappeared from the doorway with a portable keg of beer in tow.

"Stakeout refreshment," Rusty exclaimed, tossing down the barrel.

Rusty set up the keg between them as they settled in to wait. Rusty quickly downed enough drinks to kill a small horse and then he passed out in his comfortable chair. Jack didn't mind. It was probably better for everyone if the short sarcastic man avoided this fight. Jack peered out the window, watching for any sign of movement. Nothing outside stirred, other than a few bunny rabbits, and they weren't going to hurt anybody.

Just as Jack went to turn away from the window, two muffled clicks could be heard as the business end of a revolver was shoved into the small of his back.

"Why are you here?" asked a deep voice. "This isn't any of your business. Leave me alone."

"Shane, I don't want to hurt you and I'm not trying to get into your business," reasoned Jack, raising his hands in a submissive gesture. "You have some information about some people I'm looking for. The same ones that gave me this bandage on the back of my head." Jack pointed with one finger.

"I don't care about any of that stuff," answered Shane. "I want my money and I want it now."

"Rusty!" yelled Jack.

Rusty, startled awake, fell off his chair. He

looked up from the ground to see Shane holding a revolver to Jack's back.

"Uh, I see we have company. Did you offer him a drink?" asked Rusty inching to his feet.

"Rusty," warned Jack. "Not now."

"Sure, sure," Rusty pulled some money from the clip behind his beard. He placed it half way between the keg and the door. "I'll just put it on the ground here and walk away. It's all yours, Shane."

Shane poked the gun into Jack's back. He walked Jack over to the cash on the ground and forced Jack to pick it up.

"Hand it over, Jack," Shane said pushing the gun harder into his back.

Jack turned around, offering the money to the deranged gunman. As the bills were passed from one man's hand to the other's, the unmistakable sound of a double barreled shotgun cocking echoed in the room.

"You always did have good timing, brother," Rusty announced, heralding the arrival of an equally short statured, blond-haired man, standing behind Shane, with the business end of his shotgun resting between Shane's shoulder blades.

Jack smiled at Shane and began, "Now, about that information…"

CHAPTER SIX

"Caleb," exclaimed Rusty. "I was just about to --
"

Caleb interrupted him, "I know you were, brother. I'm just glad I made it in time to lend a hand."

The two stoutly built men embraced with a strong hug. Shane had been duct taped to the chair by the door. Jack made sure the restraints were tight enough to restrain an elephant. The thief wasn't going anywhere anytime soon.

While Rusty went back to the kitchen to fetch yet another keg of beer, Jack took the opportunity to thank Caleb for saving the day. Caleb and his brother were cut from different cloth; he was only a bit older but packed three times the maturity. There was no talking him into taking credit for the save. Caleb was positive he had merely shown up at the right time.

"Still," continued Jack. "Better to be lucky than dead."

"Nonsense," Caleb answered, sitting down in the nearest comfortable chair. "Everything would've worked out fine one way or the other. Why was he pointing a gun at your back, anyway?"

Rusty walked back in with another beer keg and a pitcher of water. Caleb had sworn off drinking years ago and wouldn't touch the stuff, even if someone paid him. After Jack gave Caleb a quick rundown on what he had missed, the group turned their attention toward Shane.

Rusty was no master of interrogation; he was much more likely to get angry and punch the guy right in the nose. Caleb surrounded the former thief with three chairs and as each man took a seat, sweat began forming on Shane's brow as he realized the gravity of the situation.

Caleb was a wise man. He knew the threat of violence was almost as good, if not better, than the real thing. He hummed cheerfully as he loaded the shotgun in front of their captive. Jack and Rusty stretched, warming up their shoulders and fists. A moment passed before Shane started rocking and mumbling, his eyes wide.

"All right," cried Shane as the gag was removed from his mouth, spitting out dry cotton fibers. "Whatever you want to know. Just tell me what you want to know, I'll tell you. I swear. Honest."

"Never believe a thief who uses the word 'honest,' Jack," Rusty quipped.

Jack knew better than that. Shane was going to tell the gang whatever they needed to know, and make up whatever he didn't, just to save his own skin. It was all Caleb could do to keep Rusty calm. Shane had the nerve to set Jack up on his own turf and not even offer him a bribe. Rusty considered that rude.

"I need to know who contacted you about the pendant," Jack said calmly. "Tell me everything you know and, if I believe you, we'll let you go. We'll even give you your money back."

"Sure, Jack. Whatever I can do to help. You know you can count on me," Shane continued to babble. "About a week ago, some guy comes up to me downtown. He says he has a job for me. All I have to do is convince Rusty to let me steal a pendant. The guy gives me all the details and, wouldn't you know, they were dead on. It was almost like they wanted me to steal the pendant."

Rusty slapped his forehead.

"What?!" asked Shane.

Jack stopped Rusty with his right arm, pushing him back down into the chair as he tried to get up. "Nothing. Don't worry about it. Please continue."

"Okay, well, this really old guy and a really beautiful girl are just standing around. She bends over to grab her luggage and I took the opportunity to relieve her of the pendant. But I swear the old guy saw me. I guess he didn't, because he didn't stop me."

"And that didn't strike you as odd?" Rusty interrupted again. "You're about as swift as an ox in molasses."

Caleb poured another beer and slammed it into Rusty's chest. "Drink up, brother."

"Look, some guy offered me a lot of money to take some broad's pendant and that's what I did," Shane argued. "What more do you want from me? And why do you care?"

"Because whoever gave you that information did it as a set up to give me a message," Jack responded. "I got the message loud and clear. Now I want to know how to send my response."

"Oh, I get it," Shane said with a smile. "You need my help. Okay, I'll tell you where to find this guy. He gave me an address in case there were any problems. I'll tell you where it is. For a fee."

Rusty spit out his beer and leaped to his feet. "Why you little…" Caleb and Jack both pushed him back down into the chair.

"Information first, Shane," Jack said with one fist clenched and the other holding his redheaded buddy down in his chair. "Give me something that I can use to find these people and then I'll get you your money."

"Okay. All you need to do is go down to the Star Lake strip club," Shane announced with a proud expression. "The guy said to ask at the bar for Vincent and to say I need to do my laundry."

The group all looked at each other at the same time with the same expression, as if to say "is this guy serious?"

"One of you needs to stay here and babysit our new friend," Jack said to the others. "We can't let this weasel go back to his masters. For all we know, he is still in on it." Jack tossed his coat on and nearly punched a hole through the pocket looking for the keys to his Jeep.

"Jack, Sonja still works down there," Rusty said putting a hand on Jack's back. "I can go talk to this Vincent. You don't need to go."

"Yes, I do, Rusty," Jack said, shrugging off Rusty's comforting gesture. "I'm the one who was given the message. I need to be the one to deliver the response."

"I'll stay here and guard of our troublesome friend," Caleb patted the shotgun. "He shouldn't be any trouble."

Jack ran outside, jumped over the corner of his Jeep and slid across the hood. His feet didn't seem to even touch the ground as Jack swung open the door and jumped inside. With a turn of the key, the old Jeep's engine started purring. He put it in drive just as the passenger side door swung open. Jack was already peeling out of from the front of the shop when Rusty hopped into the passenger seat.

"Let's go already," laughed Rusty. "You drive like my grandmother."

Jack shook his head in amused disbelief. The Jeep veered from left to right, weaving around the other cars on the road. The engine roared as Jack held down the gas pedal. They sped across several intersections, nearly being T-boned at each one. Jack's mind wasn't on the road.

Sonja Krenzky was a beautiful Russian with jet black hair and legs from here till Sunday. She had immigrated with her parents when she was just a baby. Jack could hardly recognize her accent; it was nearly indistinguishable, but he knew it well. It was the kind of voice that sent shivers up a man's spine. The combination of looks and sound that could get a man killed. In Jack's case, it almost had.

CHAPTER SEVEN

Five years ago, Jack had been working a case involving arson. Someone was torching some of the most antique places in the entire town. The police were clueless. At every new crime scene the police officers found a map, which would always point to the next building that would be burned. Sonja was a volunteer firefighter. She loved the town and wanted to help keep it in tip top shape. She loved the people, loved helping others and loved showing up the guys. Sonja was a firecracker, all right. One day, when the engine arrived on scene, Sonja was the one to find the map. She was sick of someone torching the town she loved and wasn't going to stand for it anymore.

Meanwhile, Jack was tracking down stolen property. Rusty kept him informed of all of the goods that were supposed to have been burned up in each building, which were mysteriously showing up in his shop. Jack got a tip from Rusty that the next house being whispered about was the old mill on 22nd.

Both Jack and Sonja had the same idea, but neither one knew it. Jack arrived in back of the building and entered through some old storm doors.

The doors were ancient, but he was able to pry them open with the right amount of force. He swept through the property, but there was no sign of the perpetrator, or anyone else for that matter.

Jack froze when he heard a knock against the outside wall. He ran to the second story, ready to catch the criminal. He saw a shadowy figure entering through a broken window, rolling onto the floor. Before the figure had a chance to right itself, Jack pounced at the criminal. They rolled end over end, breaking termite ridden furniture along the way.

"Just give up," Jack yelled. "I've got you."

"No, you don't," said the sweetest voice Jack had ever heard.

The figure tossed Jack up and over with a thrust of her powerful legs. Jack crashed right through an old table. Dazed, Jack shook it off only to see a pair of long legs in torn jeans standing over him.

"Finally," she said. "Your days of burning our buildings are over."

"Whoa," said Jack. "I'm not the criminal. You are."

She squatted down over his chest and leaned into the light shining on Jack's head. "Do you see this," she asked pointing to her firefighter's badge on her navy blue shirt. Her chest rose and fell beneath it, breathing hard from the tussle. "That means I'm the good woman and you're the bad guy."

"No way," Jack argued looking up, pinned in the trap of her legs. "You just broke through a second story window."

"It was already broken, thank you," she huffed.

An explosion roared, not more than two rooms away, and the building shook, sending the two sprawling to the floor. A fireball tore through the room, clinging to the ceiling, leaving glowing orange embers in its wake. Fire began spreading, lighting up the room they were in. Sonja scrambled to her feet pushing off Jack's chest. She helped Jack up and they both took off, running through the corridors. The walls were caving in fast. The old mill couldn't take a severe thunderstorm, let alone such an explosion.

They made it to the other side of the building where Jack grabbed the nearest rusted piece of metal and launched it straight through the glass window. He looked behind him to see Sonja pushing him along.

"Let's go," she said in a calm tone that belied the alarm on her face.

The fire shot up both sides of the walls, enveloping the doorway. The ceiling moaned and groaned as the floor beneath them cracked. Jack stepped out of the window and onto the ledge. The ceiling groaned once more and with a loud crash the contents of the room above came falling toward them. Sonja was pinned under the rubble as the flames reached toward the window. Jack jumped back in, breathing as shallowly as he could. He strained with all his might, but Sonja was stuck under a large piece of ceiling tile.

"Go. Get out of here," she screamed at the top of her lungs, coughing dirt.

Jack reached into the flames two feet away for a steel bar that had fallen through the ceiling. Heat radiated from it, and he wrapped his shirt around his hand before he grabbed the steel bar. He placed it on the edge of the tile, directly under the corner. Jack heaved with everything he had, managing to split the tile right down the center. Reaching for Sonja's hands, Jack pulled her out from under the rubble. The momentum made him stumble backward, Sonja falling forward. The floor cracked underneath their feet, revealing the raging fire on the first floor.

Jack's momentum carried him right through the window. They tumbled onto the ledge, Jack rolling and slipping right off the edge. Fortunately, Jack still had a hold of Sonja's arm as she hooked her foot into the gutter. The remaining windows blew out with tremendous force, pushing her foot off the ledge.

When the emergency crews arrived on scene, they found Jack lying on his back with Sonja sprawled out on top of him. They had landed on years of unclipped shrubbery and bushes, which had broken their fall. Right next to them was a pile of rubble, including points of sharp barbed wire, a man in a ski mask crushed underneath.

Days later, when Jack and Sonja woke up in the hospital, they were formally introduced. It wasn't love at first sight. They argued for hours over who had saved the other. It didn't matter. Ultimately, they had solved the case and saved the town. Everybody won.

After years of a passionate but volatile relationship, the two decided to call it quits. Namely, Sonja decided it was time to call it quits. Jack was heartbroken, even if he wouldn't show it to anyone else. Rusty knew. He had been Jack's friend for as long as either could remember. Best friends just knew that kind of thing.

"Jack," said Rusty. "We're here. Snap out of it."

Jack slapped the sides of his face, as if to wake himself up.

"Let's go," Jack said.

As they walked into the Star Lake Club, the world on the outside seemed to disappear. Gorgeous dancers in old-fashioned hanging cages danced on either side of the door, greeting the men as they walked in. It was an old place, visibly so from the outside, but on the inside there was nothing but wall-to-wall red velvet. All of the furniture was upholstered in red velvet and all of the dancers wore red outfits--at least the ones who were still wearing clothes, anyway.

The duo walked straight up to the bar. The light-haired bartender was busy serving another customer at the other end of the bar. Jack let out a sigh of relief. He knew it would be much easier if he didn't have to see Sonja.

The unmistakable sound of bottles clanging together sounded from the other side of the counter.

"Hey, Eddie," a soft voice yelled. "We have plenty of vodka," she continued, a head of long, cascading jet black hair popping up from behind the bar. "See, right--" She stopped mid-sentence. The beautiful woman behind the bar paused to collect herself before addressing the man before her with a degree of surprise in her voice. "Jack."

"Hi, Sonja," Jack replied. "Been a long time."

CHAPTER EIGHT

"I think I'll just... yeah..." Rusty said, backing away from the bar turning and towards the dancers.

"Yep, it's been a while, Jack," Sonja said, grabbing a shot glass and placing it on the counter in front of him. She poured him his favorite whiskey and set the bottle down beside the shot glass.

Jack took the shot and threw it back with the expertise of an alcoholic. The whiskey tasted sweeter somehow. His heart was starting to pound. He was having trouble thinking. Jack reminded himself he was there on business, he didn't have time to rehash old memories or to start beating dead horses, again.

"Right. I'm looking for a guy named Vincent. Do you know where I might be able to find him?" Jack asked in a very matter-of-fact kind of way, trying to hide any emotion he may have for the dark-haired temptress.

"He's a little busy, right now. What do you need?" she asked, tossing the towel from her shoulder on the counter.

"It's about some business ventures of his that went wrong. I'm here to help correct that," he said, pouring another shot. Sonja's face wrinkled, her eyes narrowed.

"Sure, Jack, come with me. He's in the back," she said snatching the drink right out from under his lips. Jack wanted to protest, but he knew better. There was nothing like trying to reason with an angry woman in his opinion; especially when he was clueless about what he had done.

Sonja stomped to the end of the bar and let herself out. She stood at the corner of the wall waiting to walk down a dark hallway in the corner of the room where no one looked.

Jack went to signal for Rusty, but as he turned around to find his trusty companion, he noticed the redheaded man was already on stage with a boa around his neck being entertained by three dancers. He didn't get to be the head of the thieves' guild without having a boatload of charm, which was currently being used on the girls. The audio system blared a slow song, the women getting extra close, swinging their hips in time to the music. Jack shook his head at Rusty as he tried groping a few, only to be slapped by the giggling girls. He decided to keep walking.

Sonja was standing with her arms crossed waiting to escort him to his destination. As they walked down the hallway he couldn't help but notice the main bar was well lit and colored red wall-to-wall, yet this hallway was black but not dim.

"Kind of strange location for a manager's office," remarked Jack.

Sonja knocked on the door at the end of the

hallway leaning up against the frame. "Vince, you have company," she said, glaring at Jack.

"Who? What do they want? If it ain't money, I ain't interested," said a deep voice from behind the door.

"He says it's about business," she said, pausing before opening the door.

"Well, well. If it ain't the Finder himself. Hows you doin' Mr. Finder," the man said, sitting with his feet up and crossed on a giant oak desk.

The office was relatively small and filled with filing cabinets stuffed to the brim with pieces of paper. The office itself was well lit and smelled like a place where air fresheners go to die. On the front edge of the middle of the desk sat a small plaque reading: Vincent Hardy, Boss.

Although he had never met one, Jack had heard of the so-called bosses. They were supposed to be the invisible enforcers of the town, their henchmen offering protection to local businesses, running drug rings, and controlling the underground market.

Meanwhile, the real puppet masters referred to themselves as the Syndicate. They made the decisions that mattered to the big picture. They controlled who won the local elections, what business permits were approved and which people needed to disappear. Everyone who was anyone in town owed it to the Syndicate.

Bosses were used to handle the things that the Syndicate considered trivial, and kept a fragile peace with the police, the thieves' guild and each other.

44

Vincent was an average sized, middle-aged man, with more hair above his lip than on his head. His freshly-shined shoes were a horrible match for the brown slacks and stained undershirt that completed with the ensemble. He wore a short red tie with a golden falcon pin attached to his lapel.

It was hard to tell if the yellow light that filled the room was from the layers of pollution from his cigars or the reflection from his toothbrush-forsaken teeth. Either way, the smell of ash, booze and sweat turned Jack's stomach upside down.

Jack knew the scoundrel was showing signs of intimidation masked by overconfidence. He decided the best approach was to be aggressive and demand information. "I was given word by one of your... what would you call them--specialists--that your name was mentioned as the person to go to when something went wrong regarding a recent business venture," he said sitting down on the cleanest chair of the two sitting in front of the giant oak desk.

"I have no idea what you mean," he responded putting his feet down on the ground and leaning forward toward Jack. "I'm the owner of this here establishment."

Sonja closed the door behind Jack and took a seat on the edge of the couch with her arms still folded. Jack could feel her glare on the back of his neck. He didn't need the extra pressure of an ex-girlfriend looking down on him in the middle of finding out who wanted him out of the retrieval business.

"Just tell him what he needs to know, Vince,"

45

she said with contempt. "So then he can be on his way."

"Sure thing, sugar," Vincent responded with the same vigor as a poodle who was being commanded by his master. "She has quite the way of getting what she wants. You know what I mean?"

Jack knew all too well. "I have an idea," he said nodding in agreement. "A friend of yours named Shane says you were the point of contact on the necklace job."

The color instantly drained out of Vincent's face. "Shane talks too much," he said, reaching for a sweat rag to dry his forehead. "Look, I didn't have nothing to do with that job. Some tall muscle type came in here and wanted me to steal a necklace. I told him I ain't in that line of work no more."

Vincent stood from behind the desk and walked over to Sonja, putting his arm around her shoulder. "I have a good thing going here," he said smiling. "I ain't gonna mess it up goin' back now. I knew Shane was still in the business, so I gave him the job. Simple as that."

Sonja shrugged off his advances and stood up, moving over to the other side of the room. She started rummaging through one of the dusty filing cabinets, tossing paper after paper out of her way. After a minute, she stumbled on a business card stained with coffee, which had an address written on the back. "That same muscle-bound jerk shoved this down my top yesterday after sucking down a shot he ordered and didn't pay for," she said with all the feistiness Jack remembered.

"He told me I could meet him there if I really wanted to be paid," she gagged.

Jack took the business card from her and examined the address. It looked to be in the same section of town where he woke up with a fresh bandage on his head. That side of town was rundown in the harshest sense of the word, but also full of all the elements that kept him in business. There were areas down there that even Rusty wouldn't visit alone.

"Thanks, Sonja," Jack said looking into her eyes for the first time since they had met again. "I'm going to go find this guy and tell him he needs to pay for that drink."

Sonja let out the first half smile Jack had seen since entering the place. She blushed and looked at the ground before walking towards the door. Jack took his cue and started walking. As the pair walked down the hallway he remembered all the good times. He couldn't remember what went wrong and why they weren't still together.

He slowed his pace and stopped right before entering the main part of the building. "Do they treat you well here?" he asked turning towards her.

"Yes. Vince is a good guy. He stops all the creeps who think I'm on the menu," she said with more of a smile this time. "I'm okay. Don't worry."

"I am worried," Jack said. "You don't need to be in a place like this."

The expression on her face changed for the worse. "I'm a big girl, Jack," she answered, her annoyed tone returning. "Why don't you just go find your next missing person and let me worry about myself?"

Her words hit him like a shot to the gut. One minute it felt like she was starting to come around, maybe ready to re-live the old times, the next it was like those times never happened. He knew she was tired of all the cases, all the nights alone and all the times he came home only to tell her stories of how he almost hadn't come home. But it didn't stop him from missing her.

"Waaaaahooooooo," Jack walked away from Sonja's frosty stance and walked toward the noise. As he approached the main bar, he could see Rusty dancing with two of the girls, both of whom had more of their clothes on the floor of the stage than on their bodies.

He got about halfway to the front door before Rusty realized Jack was leaving. "Gah," he exclaimed. "I'm sorry, girls, I've got to get going."

"No! Stay," Mandy and Kandy, twins from some town in the middle of nowhere, which Rusty had already forgotten the name of, said in protest. He slapped both of them on the rear assuring them he'd return later. Rusty jumped off the stage and caught up to Jack.

The sun still slept as they hastened toward the Jeep, and Jack wasn't about to go to that part of town without a small army at that time of night. Jack told Rusty what had happened with Vince and Sonja. They decided it was a better idea to go back to the shop and let the investigation wait until morning.

48

It was extremely quiet around Rusty's business. One of the perks of being high up in the Guild of Thieves was that he didn't have to worry about the night time riffraff. No one was going to mess with the guy in charge, unless there was good money in it. After parking the Jeep, Jack noticed that the lights were out inside. Without a word, Jack and Rusty both exited the vehicle and rushed up to the door.

The two stood on either side of the entrance, with their backs against the wall. Jack did some complicated army-style hand gestures and Rusty nodded. Jack reached across and opened the door. Rusty paused and stuck his head in for quick peek; he shook his head. Jack darted into the room and ducked into the shadows with Rusty close behind.

CHAPTER NINE

Inside it was pitch black. The bare floorboards were illuminated by the moonlight that filtered through the windows. Neither Rusty or Jack could see anything out of place, but for all they knew there could have been a lion waiting in the dark; they wouldn't have seen it until it was eating them for a late night snack. Jack stood up from his crouched position and hit the light switch.

"Caleb!" Rusty bellowed, running over to a body lying on the floor. He knelt down beside his brother and rolled him from a curled up position onto his back . Caleb groaned as his body fell back. Rusty looked all around, but couldn't see any signs of blood.

"Caleb," Rusty put his hands on his brother's shoulders. "Wake up. This is no time for a nap."

"What happened?" Caleb asked as he sat up slowly. He blinked repeatedly, stretching his neck from side to side. He wiped his mouth, removing the taste of the floor from his lips.

"I was just about to ask you the same thing," responded Rusty pushing up off the ground.

Rusty helped his brother up to his feet. Caleb was shaky at first, but regained his composure as quickly as could be expected. The brothers walked over to Jack, who was kneeling beside Shane. He was face down, arms limp at his sides.

"My head is killing me," Caleb said, rubbing a tender spot as they approached. "I feel like I was hit with the blunt end of a rifle. Is our troublemaker awake?"

"I don't think he'll be causing anyone any more trouble," Jack said rising to reveal the pool of blood on the ground underneath Shane's body. "I don't understand. How did they know?"

"I don't know, Jack," Caleb took a seat in a nearby chair. "Not ten minutes ago, the lights flickered and suddenly went out. I got up to check the fuse box, but I didn't get more than a couple of steps -the next thing I remember Rusty was telling me to wake up."

"It's all right, Caleb," Jack took a seat next to him, one arm around Caleb's shoulders, patting his arm. "There was nothing you could do. Rusty, get on the phone and call the cops. Tell them we have a fresh body for the morgue."

Rusty got up and went toward the back of the building and while he was gone, the sound of tires screeching came from outside. Jack knew there could be no way the cops had arrived that quickly, not in his town. He jumped up and stood, ready, beside the door. Caleb reached for his trusty double-barreled shotgun, still loaded from earlier, which he pointed at the door from his chair.

The sound of the running engine slowed then faded as whatever vehicle that had been so quick to arrive pulled away. A moment later there was a soft knock at the door. Jack looked through the peep hole, but the only thing he could see was long black hair. He opened the door a crack at first and then threw it wide open.

"Jack," Sonja clutched the door frame, shaking, with her head down. Her left arm was holding her stomach. The sleeves of her shirt had been torn. Jack could see tear stains on her reddened cheeks, beneath her half closed left eye.

"Sonja!" Jack caught her as she fell through the doorway. He scooped her up into his arms and carried her to the couch. Jack placed a pillow under her head and sat down on the coffee table beside the couch next to her. Rusty walked back into the room, oblivious to the commotion.

"What happened?" Rusty asked alarmed by the sight of his best friend's ex, semi-conscious on his couch. Caleb and Rusty both moved behind the couch looking down over the injured woman they had both known for years. "That looks like blood on her shoes."

"Is she bleeding?" Caleb asked with trepidation.

"Not that I can see," Jack reached for Sonja's hand. "Hon, can you hear me?"

She groaned, out of it, but nodded slightly. She opened her eyes to see the bearded twins standing above her with worried expressions.

"I'm okay," she said, sitting up slowly, wincing in pain.

She took a deep breath. Her eyes widened, staring into the distance. "They came in right after you left. Not a minute after you left. There must've been a dozen, I couldn't see them, and we didn't know what was happening. Vince tried. He really tried. I can't believe this--"

"Hon," Jack said in a calming voice, the best he could muster when seeing someone he cared about in so much pain. "Slow down. Tell us what happened."

Sonja took three deep breaths. "Right after you left, a dozen men dressed all in black stormed into the club. They shot our bouncer twice in the chest. The girls ran into the dressing room, screaming. One of the men rushed the bar and grabbed me by the arm. I punched him as hard as I could but, before I knew it, three others were on me. There wasn't anything I could do."

"You did fine," Jack soothed, trying his best to hide his anger. "You got out of there and you're safe."

"No," she yelled. "Another one dragged Vince out from the back. They wanted to know what he'd told you. He wouldn't tell them, but when he wouldn't talk, even after they hit him, one of them hit me. He tried to stop him. He did. He broke down and told them what happened," she paused. "They shot him! Why would they shoot him? He answered all of their questions," she began to sob.

Rusty leaned over the back of the couch, gently patting the back of her shoulder. "How did you escape?"

"I'm not sure," she said, drying her tears with the back of her hand. "One of the ones near the door yelled and they all marched out."

"Jack," Caleb said, moving toward the window by the door. He flipped the light switch, sending them into darkness. "I bet they're on their way. We need to get out of here, now."

"Can you move?" Jack said to Sonja with a hand outstretched to her. He couldn't help but stare at her, feeling responsible. If he hadn't gone to the club, she would have been spared such violence. He was angry, but he was scared for her. Jack knew Caleb was right. They needed to leave. He had to get Sonja to safety.

She took his hand and they both stood up. "I think so."

Without a sound, multiple beams of light burst through the windows. Several sets of headlights had been turned on outside. "Jack," Caleb looked out the window at three black sedans with their lights trained on the front door. "Those aren't cop cars."

A tall figure got out of one of the front cars and motioned towards the others. In the blink of an eye, the cars unloaded. More than a dozen shadowy figures, with what looked like semiautomatic weapons, stood outside Rusty's shop. The leader motioned to the left and the right. A few members of the squad broke off from the main pack and started heading around the building on either side.

"I hope you have a plan," Caleb looked at Jack.

"He always has a plan," Rusty answered with confidence. "Right, Jack?"

"Jack," a loud voice, projected through a megaphone outside. "We can do this the easy way.

54

Come out and no one gets hurt."

If there was one thing that Jack knew from working in the business, it was that anyone who said "no one gets hurt" actually meant "we are going to kill you all."

CHAPTER TEN

Jack figured the men who had killed Vince and beaten Sonja were now surrounding Rusty's place with every intention of letting no one leave alive.

He had been in similar situations many times before, but it had never been so close to home, and certainly not with his friends in so much danger. He felt horrible. The only reason they were in such a mess was because of him. But there was no time for thinking like that; he needed to find a way out--and fast.

In an instant, the room went pitch black without any lights coming from the cars outside. Only small spots of light came shining through the windows, cast from the flashlights of the dark figures walking around the building. Without any hesitation, Jack shimmied his way between the beams of light. If they were going to get out, he couldn't risk the bad guys knowing which way they had gone. Once he reached the windowless room where Rusty kept his precious beer kegs, it was safe to move about more freely.

Feeling his way through the dark, Jack found the door the thieves used to escape underground, whenever the cops showed up through the front door. It was sealed by a thick layer of dust, as if it hadn't been used in quite a while.

He pried open the door. The force sent dust through the air and into his face. Decades of cobwebs tasted just as bad as fresh dirt. Jack peered down inside the floor. There was a faint sign of moonlight coming in from the outside world. The door led to a crude tunnel held up by termite-ridden beams. A few spiders and other creepy crawlies darted around, startled by the sudden movement of the door.

Jack knew it was the only way out, but if the men caught them at the other end of the tunnel, they would be forced to fight for their lives. He pondered whether they would know about the escape route. It didn't matter; it was the best option they had.

Jack made his way back to the others, being careful to dodge the beams of light. He tapped Rusty on the shoulder from behind the couch and motioned for Caleb to follow. Sonja was still shaking and barely able to walk; Jack fell down hugging the ground. He began crawling one arm over the other until he reached her. Once the lights were focused on the opposite side of the room, Jack scooped her up in a fireman's lift and ran for the storage area.

One by one the group headed down into the tunnel. Caleb and Rusty went down into the tunnel first. The sound of the front door breaking open echoed through the hallway as Jack set Sonja down with her legs dangling over the edge of the underground door frame. He could hear the footsteps crashing through the shop, approaching, as she slipped down into the tunnel. With one fluid movement, Jack slithered into the open air of the tunnel entrance, grabbing the handle on the inside of the door on the way down. The hidden door slammed behind him just as the men entered the room.

They could hear the men up above stomping their feet on the wooden floor and looking for any signs of their escape. Jack wasn't about to wait around and see if they would figure it out. He led the group down the tunnel by following the moonlight in the distance.

Jack carried Sonja the whole way. Adrenaline and fear filled him with energy and strength. He did his best to lead by example. If he showed fear, the others would be afraid as well and that wouldn't help the situation.

Rats skittered in the shadows at either side of them as they trudged onward. After what felt like an eternity, the group arrived at the end of the tunnel. Jack and Caleb took to the corners where the make-shift walls ended. They poked their heads out, scanning for signs of the men. The coast was clear.

The tunnel exit was well hidden by leafy green bushes and piles of mud, at the bottom of a large hill with 15 feet of dirt and trees sloping above them. The town's only river was 100 yards away, with nothing but freedom on the other side. The group trudged along through the mud and across the river. They kept moving for another hundred feet before finding a dry spot to catch their breath.

"I can't believe we got away clean," Caleb said, breaking the silence.

"Clean?" asked Rusty, wiping the dirt off his face and from his beard. "I wouldn't exactly be saying clean."

Caleb chuckled with his infectious laugh. It brought much-needed levity to a very serious situation. They knew the gravity of the predicament they were in. These men had gone from offering Jack a career change to trying to put him on a permanent vacation to the sweet hereafter.

Jack pulled out the business card Sonja had given him in Vince's office just a few hours earlier. He could only see two ways out of the situation. Either they could run as fast and far away from that town as possible and spend the rest of their lives wondering if they would ever be found by the Syndicate, living their lives in fear. Or Jack could confront them head on.

"What are you thinking, Jack," Sonja said knowing full well the expression on his face meant he was about to do something stupid.

"I need to pay them a visit," he said handing her back the card. "We can't run forever. I need to deal with this, once and for all. Rusty, look after Sonja. Caleb, make sure Rusty stays out of trouble."

Sonja pushed off the ground, rising to her feet. Her legs were still trembling ever so slightly beneath the skin tight, mud slathered, ripped jeans. She tore the remainder of her sleeve off her shirt and threw it on the ground.

"I'm going with you," she said with a

combination of determination, anger and fear.

Jack wanted to argue. He wanted to tell her not to, that he still cared too much and that he wouldn't be able to live with himself if something ever happened to her. But he knew better; he knew that determined look on her face. She was going to get in the middle of things, with or without him.

"Let's go," shouted Rusty and Caleb who were already heading back in the direction of town. Sonja stood with Jack for another moment. They had always shared the ability to communicate entire conversations with nothing more than a few glances. As they stood there, looking into each other's eyes, it was as if they were making up for the distance that had grown between them.

Sonja gave another half-smile before turning to catch up with the short figures in the distance.

The decision to confront the powers-that-be at the Syndicate was the only one that made sense to any of them. If they ran, the Syndicate would find them. If they fought the goons and won, the Syndicate would just send more men. The only option was to find the person who started the mess in the first place.

Tired and hurting, they marched along the river to the old bridge that served as the entrance to the town. The sun was coming up in the distance, over the mountains that stood watch over the town. The orange glow on the horizon was a beautiful sight, the highlight of an otherwise abysmal day.

There was only one familiar place between where they were, at the edge of town and the address on the business card. Sonja's sister had an apartment in the lower-middle class section of town. It wasn't fancy, but it was somewhere they could go to rest for an hour or five.

CHAPTER ELEVEN

Sonja's sister, Marge Loza, had an American last name thanks to her husband, Tom. Marge was a seamstress who worked on the garments of the upper class. Tom Loza was a shoe salesman. Between the two of them, they were barely making ends meet. They kept a small but tidy fourth floor apartment. The Lozas were out of town at a convention. Sonja hoped that by the time her family returned, the situation would be long over and they would be out of danger; besides, no one really knew the two were related. They saw each other at Christmas and other holidays, but otherwise led completely separate lives.

Rusty was more than happy to use his skeleton key, which was really nothing more than two wires bent at different angles. Lock-picking skills certainly came in handy; there was no need to raise suspicion if you can walk right in.

The apartment door swung open with just a few twists of Rusty's "key". The group filed in one by one with Jack in the rear. The small kitchen on the right already had one less beer, thanks to Rusty's raiding of the refrigerator. The living room was off to the left, set up with secondhand furniture that had seen better days. The gold silk curtains over the window, however, were of top caliber. Marge had gotten them from one of her clients with a few small holes in them, nothing that someone with her skill couldn't repair.

Caleb flopped down on the soft green couch stationed in the living room and promptly fell asleep. Rusty was more than happy to relieve the apartment of as much alcoholic refreshment as he could find in the kitchen, not to mention a roast beef sandwich and some pickles.

The room behind the living room served as the bedroom and master bathroom. In an apartment that small, space was a luxury they couldn't afford. The queen-size bed set firmly against one wall was made up with dark blue satin sheets, complete with neat hospital corners. There was a large old chest of drawers on the opposite wall by the window, nestled beside a well-used sewing table.

The master bathroom was too small to really be called master, but it was big enough to hold a bathtub with a slightly rusted overhead shower, a small sink with a mirrored medicine cabinet and a small commode. The only luxury item in the bathroom was a full-length mirror, set in an oval wooden frame. It was a family heirloom, extremely old, but well taken care of.

Jack walked over to the bed and sat down next to the nightstand. His mind was racing with worry about what would happen in the hours to come. They would be taking on a large and powerful group of men, who stole and killed for living. The question of how they would get in, if he could keep everyone safe and what they would do once they got inside swam around his head.

The sound of the shower turning on snapped Jack out of the dark place his mind was going. He needed to relax, and stressing about what was to come wasn't going to do any good. The slightly off-key singing coming from the shower was familiar and comforting. It had been a long time since he had heard Sonja sing.

Leaning down to release his sore foot from his left boot, he caught a glimpse of Sonja's leg resting on the edge of the bathtub in the oval mirror. It was foggy from the steam of the shower and the shower curtain was drawn for privacy, hiding most of her, except for the leg she was sticking out on the ledge to clean.

Jack lay back on the bed with his arms crossed behind his head and his feet crossed at the other end. It all brought back a flood of memories of times gone by. He and Sonja never had the chance to resolve what had happened between the two of them. He wanted to tell her he would change, stop chasing bad guys or whatever it took before everything came crashing down, but he had let that moment fly by, like so many others he had come to regret. He began to wonder if they could work things out after everything was settled.

A moment later Sonja walked out of the bathroom, a full-length pink towel around her glistening skin, drying her hair with a smaller towel on her head.

"You don't have to do this," said Jack.

"Yes, I do," she answered smirking. "I don't like wet hair."

Jack gave her a scowl. "You know what I mean."

"I know," she said walking over to the side of the bed. She sat down beside him, mouth closed and lip stiff, staring into his eyes.

"Thank you," he said putting his hand on her shoulder.

She smiled at him and patted his hand then continued drying her hair. As she finished drying she happened to catch a glance at the mirror and the reflection of the bathtub in it. Sonja looked at the reflection and then back at Jack.

"Were you watching me in that mirror?" she asked.

"Why, I never," he said as dignified as he could. "How could you even think I would?"

Sonja interrupted his speech by beating him with the towel in her hand.

"Okay. Okay," he said laughing and covering his head. She continued on, giggling and smacking him around. She fell on him without ceasing the assault until he cried truce.

Sonja stood up from the bed, but not before giving him one more good smack with the towel. She went to the chest of drawers to find something to wear. The clothes she had removed were torn and muddy, nothing she could wear back in town without attracting unwanted attention. She grabbed a black T-shirt and a pair of brown pants from the drawer before retreating to the bathroom. A hand appeared around the door clutching a towel which was tossed at Jack's head. He pulled it off just in time to see the door shut.

Smiling to himself, he felt good enjoying her company again. He missed how playful she was. She smelled like roses dipped in cinnamon, but when her arm brushed his lips it tasted more like honey. He started imagining the view he would have had if the mirror hadn't been so foggy. Just when he was about halfway into a good daydream, a noise from the other room broke his concentration.

"Rusty? Caleb? You two okay?" he yelled to the other room. When no one answered, he tossed his legs over the side of the bed, sliding his feet back into his boots.

He stood up and went to the other room. There was no sign of either of them. Figuring Rusty was still raiding the refrigerator, he decided to look in the kitchen.

"We should get some food before we go," Sonja said tucking in her shirt as she opened the door from the bathroom, only to find an empty bed.

"Jack? Guys?" she yelled into the other room, to no response. "Where are you guys?"

She walked from the bedroom through the living room and out toward the kitchen, when she noticed a pair of legs on the floor. Those are Jack's boots, she thought to herself, right before she felt the pinch of a syringe needle sinking into her neck.

"Shhh. Go to sleep," said a male voice from

behind Sonja.

She wanted to run and scream. She wanted to do anything, but her body wouldn't cooperate. The man put his arm around her waist to catch her as she fell. He eased her to the ground. Sonja could see Jack, Rusty and Caleb, passed out in the kitchen, just as everything went dark.

CHAPTER TWELVE

"Sonja," said a quiet whisper. "Wake up."

She opened her eyes and focused as best she could, trying to see through her blurry vision. She could see her trusty companions lined up beside her, with their chairs facing alternate directions.

Jack was still out cold. He was bound to the chair right beside her. His hands were wrapped with a triple layer of taut rope. She saw Rusty and Caleb squirming to get out of the same kind of ties on the other side of Jack.

"Where are we?" she asked, her head still feeling fuzzy from the drugs.

A strong thick rope bound Sonja's hands together behind her chair while her feet were bound together attached to the bottom of the chair. She started struggling against the ties in a vain attempt to set herself free. The chill in the air, combined with the anxiety of the situation, sent goose bumps up and down her body.

The room was dark, but not pitch black, and a shimmering silver metal seemed to line the walls. There was one window, high up where the wall met the ceiling, on her side of the room. There was one door off to her left; it looked large and heavy, like the blast-proof door of a bunker. Whoever wanted them in that cold dark room had made sure they wouldn't be leaving anytime soon.

The stench of musk and cigarettes permeating the air, creeping into Sonja's nostrils. She was used to those scents from the gentleman's club, but they still bothered her.

"Sonja," Rusty leaned backward to peek around Caleb's head. "Can you reach him?"

She nodded and started rocking in her chair left to right. The chair shook back and forth, each sway butting up against Jack. On the final swing, her shoulder rammed into his with enough force to wake him from the drug-induced slumber.

"Ugh, my head," complained Jack.

"Jack," she said, alarmed and angry. "Wake up."

Jack shook his head violently from left to right. After a moment he scanned the room, taking stock of the situation they found themselves in. There were no windows on the side of the room he could see, but the room seemed familiar. The room had the same feel as the place he had found the pendant.

Before Jack had a chance to respond, the large metal door swung open with an almighty crash as it rebounded off the wall behind it. Two men in tailor-made suits burst through the door, armed to the teeth. They moved to either side of the door, cocked their guns and stood in a defensive position with the barrels pointed at their captives.

A large man entered the room immediately after, with another even larger man following behind. The largest man stepped to the side and leaned against the wall directly in front of Sonja. She instantly recognized his bulging muscles and the lack of a neck; he was the man who had refused to pay for his drink in the bar. His handgun was holstered on his left side, but mostly hidden behind the tree trunks that posed as his arms. His balding white boulder of a head sat atop of a steroid-built mountain of muscle.

"Happy to see me again, baby?" he said with a smirk and a wink.

Sonja desperately tried to stand. She pushed off against the floor and nearly fell forward with the momentum of her push. Her face wrinkled, eyes narrowed. Sonja tried to push off again as the adrenaline pumped through her veins. Her chair began to lift up off the floor, but quickly slammed back down, just too heavy for her to move.

"Now, now," said the deep voice of the other man, walking around in front of Jack. "We're all friends here. There's no need to get upset."

Jack got his first glimpse of the well-dressed man. The voice belonged to a tall man, six feet or more, but not particularly muscular. His suit was crafted from a fine silver material, accented with a bright purple silk tie and a white handkerchief in his left breast pocket. Jack couldn't see a gun anywhere on his person. His face was clean cut, no scars or marks. Yet his eyes showed age, experience and a glimmer of cunning.

"Your hospitality has been outstanding, so far," Jack said, looking him straight in the eye.

Rusty snickered.

"Of course," said the man. "Where are my manners? My name is Alfred Winters. It's a pleasure to meet the great finder."

"Hell of a way to meet a fan, Jack," Rusty piped up from the end of the row.

Winters glared at Rusty with his steel eyes. He snapped his fingers at the muscle-bound man. The walking rage machine pulled out a six inch serrated knife from his belt. Sonja screamed as he stepped behind Rusty. He lowered the blade, jabbing it forward and up in one fluid motion. Rusty pulled his hands free from the freshly cut rope, rubbing his wrists. The man continued down the line slicing the ropes binding each of them in a similar fashion. Once finished, the man returned to his position in front of Sonja, sheathed his blade and winked at her again.

"Pardon my overenthusiastic associate," Winters said.

"You have my attention now, Winters," Jack reached down to untie his ankles. "What did you bring us here for?"

"I have a situation that only someone of your talents can solve." Winters reached into his pocket to pull out a silvery case. He tapped on the outside of the package and opened it to reveal a dozen cigarettes. Winters extended the case out toward Jack, who shook his head. "You see, I'm the one who arranged the pendant job."

"Why would you arrange something like that?" asked Jack.

"Let's not kid each other, Mr. Finder," Winters

continued. "Your line of work can be quite troublesome to someone in my position. It takes a lot of time and planning to relieve the rich of possessions they don't need, only to have someone such as yourself give them back. It can be quite frustrating, you see."

Jack stood from his chair and took a step toward Mr. Winters. He could see, out of the corner of his eye, that the men guarding the door had their cannons pointed at his head. Winters raised an arm and motioned downward with his hand. The men lowered their weapons and return to their positions at either side of the open door.

"You're not making any sense," Jack said, confronting their captor. "You want my help, but you want me out of the business. Which is it?"

"As I'm sure you know, I'm only one of three bosses controlling this town. Unlike my peers, I see a value in what you do," Winters said, lighting his cigarette. "You could be very valuable to my organization, Mr. Finder."

"No thanks," said Jack "I don't accept job offers from people holding a gun to my head."

"I was afraid you might say that," said Winters. "No matter. If you won't accept a permanent position then perhaps you will accept my final offer. Mr. Green and I have had a rather unfortunate difference of opinion over our borders, as it were. In order to ensure my cooperation, Green kidnapped my daughter from her apartment, two days ago."

Jack raised an eyebrow staring at Mr. Winters. He could see the expression on Winters' face had changed. The man was genuinely concerned; at least as concerned as a heartless killer could be.

"If you know who did it and where she is, why don't you simply go get her yourself?" inquired Jack.

"The Syndicate would not tolerate an open war between Mr. Green and I," confessed Winters. "We would appear weak and it would only be a matter of time before the other bosses struck at both of us, in our weakened states."

"And that's where I come in," said Jack. "They would never suspect I would work for you."

"Precisely," said Winters in an excited manner. "I'm glad you understand the situation. I need for you to break into Mr. Green's hideout and get her back. This way, we avoid an open war, where dozens of innocent bystanders will be killed in the crossfire. You don't want that any more than I do, do you, Mr. Finder?"

Jack looked at Sonja and the brothers. "If I refuse?" Jack asked looking back at Winters.

"That would be extremely unfortunate," said Winters motioning to the men in the room who pointed their weapons at each of Jack's friends.

"Okay, okay," Jack responded quickly. "I'll help you. Put down the weapons."

Winters motioned again and the men went back to their positions. He smiled at Jack.

"I had a feeling you would see it my way," said Mr. Winters. "Now, you and the blond-haired one can go retrieve my daughter. I'll be keeping your beautiful lady and the loudmouth by my side until you return with Nancy, unharmed."

"I'm not leaving them with you and your knife-happy lap-dog," Jack said, motioning to the muscle-bound creep leaning against the wall.

"You have my word, Mr. Finder," continued Winters. "No harm will come to them. If Damon so much as looks at her I will shoot him myself. That is, unless you don't return in the next 24 hours. Then... well, I'm not responsible for what he does after that."

Caleb patted his brother on the arm and got up off his chair. "We'll get your daughter. Just don't hurt them," Caleb stood beside Jack.

"This isn't finished between us," Jack said, staring at Damon with his fists clenched so tight that his knuckles turned white. Damon grinned from ear to ear at Jack, patting the butt of his handgun.

"Nancy is being held at Green's hideout on 14th Street," Winters said, pulling out a small silver pocket watch. "Bring her back to me by this time tomorrow and we can all go our separate ways."

Caleb grabbed Jack by the arm and pulled him towards the door. Jack stared at Sonja, who sat with her hands clasped together, in front of her face. She was the palest he had ever seen her. Jack knew she was scared, but he was determined to get the job done and set her free. As they walked out of the room, he saw Rusty sit down beside her, patting her comfortingly on the back. She almost seemed like she was going to cry. Almost.

Jack and Caleb continued down the corridors, escorted by more well-dressed soldiers with enough artillery to take on a SWAT team. As they exited the building, Jack spotted his Jeep. It had been conveniently placed outside, with the keys still in the ignition. The two climbed into the vehicle in a hurry.

It was early in the morning, judging by where the sun was in the sky; the sound of screeching tires tore through the still air as they tore out of the parking lot. Jack knew they only had one day to scout the enemy hideout, infiltrate it and bring Nancy back alive, or he would never see Sonja's enchanting eyes again.

CHAPTER THIRTEEN

The outside of Green's hideout looked like an ordinary gray brick building; it could have been any building on any given city block. Curtained windows were on every floor and a double wide glass door served as an entryway. Jack wondered if they had been given the wrong address. The place seemed too pristine to be a hideout for one of the most vicious crime bosses in town.

Jack staked out the scene from a distance, sitting in his trusty Jeep, parked far enough away to look like it belonged. Meanwhile, Caleb checked out the building for possible gaps in security. As he walked around the building, Caleb could see the premises were well maintained. Flower boxes on either side of the entryway were planted with expensive foreign flowers that smelled like a desert island in the summer. He could almost taste the sweet juices of tropical fruit.

On the side the building, a fire escape was locked in a raised position, out of reach from the bottom floor. Surveillance cameras on every corner of the building monitored the alleyways on all sides of the building, every blind spot covered. One camera even captured the area behind the dumpster in the back of the building. Caleb could tell there wasn't a chance of them getting in without being seen.

Out by the trash was an empty pizza box from a local pizzeria, complete with grease stains and melted cheese stuck to the top. Taking the box and brushing off the extra debris, Caleb set off for the front door. He carried the box in front of him, acting as if it were heavy enough to contain food. It lacked the tantalizing odor of sizzling pepperoni, but he doubted anyone would notice over what he smelled like after the last two days without a shower.

Caleb entered through the glass doors. On the right-hand side was a wall of mailboxes twice his height and on the left was a marvel security desk, complete with a dark, menacing looking attendant. Behind the man, a mahogany door labeled "authorized personnel only" stood slightly ajar. He could see the flicker of black-and-white televisions, but it was impossible to tell if anyone was watching them.

There was only one elevator in the place and it was still on the fourth floor of the ten story building. Rather than wait, Caleb decided to take the stairs. The stairwell itself was well lit and predictably covered with security cameras. He made his way up the stairs past the second floor when the sound of one of the metal doors closing echoed through the stairwell. Caleb looked down over the railing to see the man who had been sitting at the security desk now staring up at him from the first floor.

"Where are you headed, pal?" The man's tone

was unfriendly, but the unlocked handguns holstered on either side of his chest over a dress shirt and dark pants were even more hostile.

"Tenth floor, someone ordered a pepperoni and anchovy with extra cheese," said Caleb in a tough guy accent.

"I don't think so, buddy. No one goes to the tenth floor," answered the man waving his arms.

"Hey, I was told there was a generous tip in it for me if I got this to the top floor in a hurry," Caleb continued with the bad accent.

The guard stared in silence.

Caleb's left hand quivered, the index finger stretched. He was never much for running and he wasn't about to start then.

"Hey, alright, take it yourself," said Caleb walking back down the stairs.

He handed over the pizza box, huffed and then started to head for the door. Halfway between the stairwell and the front door he heard a loud shout. "Hey," shouted the gunman. "Stop!"

Caleb froze in his tracks. The man must have discovered the pizza box was empty. Caleb was unarmed, five feet from the door, and Jack was nowhere nearby. He thought about running, but there wasn't time.

"You forgot your money, pal," he said handing Caleb a crisp $20 bill. "Keep the change. Now get out of here."

Caleb let out a sigh of relief, took the $20 bill and headed for the door. He walked down the block to where Jack had parked. As Caleb sat down in his seat, the glass doors of the apartment building flew open and six men streamed out, led by the dual-pistol wearing thug. He tossed the pizza box on the sidewalk, gesturing to the left and right of the building. He stomped on the pizza box angrily and kicked it into the street.

"Who knew the pizza delivery business was so rough," said Jack, smirking at Caleb.

"We're definitely not getting in the front door," Caleb said. "They have more security cameras than Fort Knox, Mr. Unfriendly at the front desk and the fire escapes are locked. There's only one elevator and one stairwell. Everything is covered."

"Not everything," Jack said as he started up the Jeep.

They drove down the street, past the hideout and around behind the neighboring building, which was much more rundown by comparison. The alleyway was dirty, dark and the perfect place to park a vehicle you didn't want to be seen. This time, the fire escape wasn't pinned up. Jack and Caleb headed for the ladder. Eleven stories was a long climb up for the shorter man, but a walk in the park for Jack.

Once both of them made it to the top of the building, Jack walked over to the side facing Green's hideout. He surveyed the top of both building for what seemed like an eternity.

"This is our way in. Stay here," said Jack as he took off running for the fire escape.

His feet slid down the fire escape one flight at a time until he reached the second floor. From there, he leapt down onto the closed dumpster. With another quick jump, he landed in the back of the Jeep. Jack knelt down, rummaging through the equipment he kept in his vehicle at all times.

After a few moments, Jack reappeared on top of the building. Caleb knelt down behind the brick ridge of the roof. Jack took the materials over to Caleb and dropped them at his feet. Caleb surveyed the ropes and gloves. He picked the gloves up off the ground, placing them between his teeth. The foul taste of oil residue laced Caleb's mouth and he pulled a face as he bent down, picked up one end of the rope, ran it over to the cinder-block stack-house in the middle of the roof and tied it off in a slip knot, securing it as tightly as possible.

Jack took the other end of the rope in his hand and began fastening a lasso. He had learned a lot of tricks over the years, but roping a building was never something he had practiced. The rough rope slid through his fingertips as he began the rotation in his shoulder, gearing up for the throw. Jack's eyes centered in on a large metal pipe sticking out of the roof on the other side. With the sun setting behind him, Jack tossed the lasso across the gap between the two buildings, narrowly catching his target.

Caleb nodded in approval. Jack pulled hard on the rope, securing the other end. When they were both sure the line would hold, the pair put on their gloves and prepared to cross the street, over 120 feet above the sidewalk below.

Jack went first, choosing to stand up and walk across the rope just as a tight rope walker would. He set out on the edge to start his journey, placing one foot gingerly in front of the other, time after time. Before he knew it he was half way across with no net below. He thought to himself how easy walking on a rope looked when people did it in the circus. But it wasn't the first time Jack had tiptoed on a rope to save someone or something. He hoped it wouldn't be the last, either.

Reaching the other side unseen was the ultimate goal. The cameras couldn't see above the building. As long as no one looked up from the street below or out of a window, it would be a stealth operation. A few feet from the end of the rope, Jack leapt into the air and over to the other side. Landing on his feet, Jack turned and moved back over to the rope staying low to the ground. He checked the rope to make sure it was still secure before motioning for Caleb to follow.

Caleb wasn't exactly the daredevil type. As opposed to walking, he climbed onto the rope, flipped upside down and dragged himself across. He kept his eyes closed, putting one hand in front of the other and pulling. The rope end on the taller building creaked and groaned, holding the stout man in midair. The knot slipped once, dropping the rope an inch or more, causing Caleb to grab on even tighter. He continued his way across, not wanting to be off the ground for longer than he had to be. When he finally reached the other side, Jack stretched over the edge of the building and pulled him up.

They knew leaving the rope attached to the

other building was a risk, but there was no guarantee Jack could safely re-lasso the rope in a hurry if they needed a quick getaway. The two decided to leave the rope attached and hope for the best.

Jack took his toolkit from his back pocket; he carried it everywhere, just for those types of situation. Within a minute he had unlocked the door. He slowly turned the knob and pushed the door open with one eye closed, half expecting an alarm. A minute passed without any sounds, and they ventured inside.

The lock on the 10th floor door was even less of a challenge for Jack and his lock picking skills. Once open, Jack peeked around the corner, spotting a security camera to the right, oscillating at the end of the hallway, but nothing to the left. Jack motioned with an arm still behind the door for them to move to the left. When the security camera was pointed the other way, Jack and Caleb headed down the hallway to the left.

The building had been renovated with marble hallways that carried even the slightest sound. Jack could hear voices coming from the end of the row of doors. Neither Jack nor Caleb could make out what they were talking about from such a distance, so they moved closer, door by door, until they were at the end of the hall. They took either side of the mahogany door on the left of the hallway before Jack knocked on the door.

Much to Caleb's surprise, the man he had fooled with the pizza charade opened the door. He looked out and down the hallway looking directly over Caleb's head. Jack tapped him on the shoulder.

"Hi," said Jack, before giving the man his best right hook, causing him to fall backwards into the room.

Jack followed him into the room, with Caleb close behind, closing the door. Jack tied up their new unconscious friend with a phone cord from the nearby wall. They cracked the door enough to be able to hear what was going on in the room next door.

"She stays in that room until Winters decides to cooperate," said a male voice. "You know the boss won't be happy if another pizza boy gets in here."

"All she wants is a drink," said another male. "Just grab her one, will ya?"

"Fine," said the first voice.

The door at the end of the hall swung open, slamming against the wall. Jack ducked around the corner, keeping the door open enough to watch one man pass by. As soon as he got down to the end of the hallway, Jack and Caleb rushed into the unlocked room.

Nancy was being held in the bedroom of one of the fanciest suites they had ever seen. A crystal chandelier hung over a glass table in the middle of the room. A man sat on on a long pink couch, his back to the door, watching television. The room wasn't large and it only took a few steps to reach the lounging man before he noticed it wasn't his peer, returning with a drink. Jack moved up to the soft fabric couch and threw his arm around the man's throat. Jack squeezed with all his might as the man threw his legs up in the air and back down again, smashing the table below the chandelier.

"Shhhh," whispered Jack as the man slumped over to the side, passed out.

Just as Jack was setting the man down on the couch, his partner returned with a glass of water in one hand and a bucket of ice in the other. Seeing Jack bent over the couch, the taller kidnapper let go of both his glass and bucket. He reached for his holstered gun on the right side of his body. The crash of glass breaking echoed down the hall accompanied by a loud metallic thud. The goon hadn't noticed Caleb crouching beside the door. His gun made it half way out of the holster before a swift uppercut between the man's legs sent him crumbling to the floor.

Caleb reached for the bucket, grabbing it by the handle and swung for the man's head. Jack jumped up from the couch and looked over at Caleb who was standing over the man with the bucket in his hand. Satisfied that both men would be sedated for the next two hours, they continued into the apartment.

The bedroom was draped with silk, and littered with laced frilly doilies. Whoever had set up this room had gone to a lot of trouble to make it as girly as possible. The furniture was pink, the curtains were pink and even the area rug under the large water bed was pink. On top of silk sheets, tucked neatly around the bed, lay a young woman; she could not have been more than twenty years old and was dressed in a purple night gown with pajama bottoms. She was fast asleep, yet still gagged with satin ties around the wrists and ankles.

Jack moved to the head of the bed gently placing his hand on the young woman's shoulder while Caleb untied her feet.

"Nancy," Jack called, shaking the woman, urging her to wake up. "My name is Jack. Your father sent me. We need to leave, now."

CHAPTER FOURTEEN

Rusty's chair rocked back and forth in the same fashion as a ticking clock. Time was passing slowly in some ways, but in others the light cast through the small window near the ceiling of their cell was changing rapidly. The hours rolled by without any sign of Jack, or Winters' daughter, which only made Rusty and Sonja grow increasingly worried. A random nameless, and rather grumpy, fellow came through only once, to offer them a drink and a chance to use the facilities, only to rebind them to their wooden chairs on his way out. Beyond that, they had been alone, left to their own thoughts and paranoia.

While Rusty passed the time with nervous behavior, Sonja sat with her eyes closed, yet fully aware of what was going on around her. She wasn't the meditative type, but in her situation, she knew the only way to pass the time was to center herself and wait for the right moment. She had convinced herself that it wouldn't do any good to break loose from their bindings only to have to fight their way out through who knew how many dozens of Winters'' lackeys, and that was even if they could figure out a way to break through the steel door.

"Would you please just sit still for a few moments, while I think?" asked Sonja, growing tired of the rickety chair noise Rusty was making.

"Sorry," Rusty responded like a scolded puppy. He waited a few seconds before continuing to rock back and forth.

"Rusty!" Sonja exclaimed.

"I'm sorry," answered Rusty, even louder.

"Could you be quiet for just one minute? That's all I'm asking. Just one minute!" Sonja shouted.

"Maybe if you spent a little bit more time making noise and a little less time thinking, we would be out of here," Rusty shouted back.

"Maybe if you spent a little less time making noise and a little more time thinking, we would be out of here," she yelled.

"Yeah? Well maybe you would--" Rusty's witty remark was interrupted by the steel door swinging open and smacking against the cinderblock wall with great force.

Damon appeared in the doorway, his face red, breathing hard. He stepped forward into the room, slamming the door behind him.

"I've had it up to here with the two of you," he said making his way over to the two captives who sat side by side, facing opposite directions.

"I'm tired of waiting. I'm tired of your mouths. Your buddies went and split on you. They aren't coming back and that means you're both mine," Damon continued, leaning down right in Sonja's face, grabbing her cheeks and squishing her lips together.

Rusty rocked his chair once more, , brute force snapping the back of the chair loose from its seat.

He pushed up with all the strength in his lower legs, shoving the top of the chair right into the jaw of their captor.

Damon's head snapped back, absorbing the blow as he fell to the ground. Rusty rushed over to where he fell, leapt up into the air with full intention of landing the hard wood directly on Damon's face, but at the last second the man rolled out of the way leaving Rusty to slam into the hard floor.

"You mother--," exclaimed the large angry man, his biceps bulging. Damon flipped himself back onto his feet and charged over to Rusty, who lay stunned on the floor. His boot drew back and followed through to Rusty's stomach. The assault continued with another kick and then another.

"Stop it!" screamed Sonja repeatedly, as she struggled to break the rope that held her down.

Her cries for mercy for her short, brave friend worked. Damon's attention turned away from Rusty and onto her. He pushed her chair backwards and climbed on top of her lap. Hunched over, he started pinching her cheeks with one hand while the other reached for his knife tucked away in his belt. His face lowered down. His breath smelled of a foul combination: rotten meat and bourbon. She shrieked and squirmed as his lips neared hers.

Sonja screamed again. Suddenly, the door swung open again, a man rushing in and heading straight for her. He grabbed Damon by the shoulders, pulling him back a few inches. Knife in hand, Damon took an underhanded swing at the man, allowing the blade to connect with the man's chest. The dazed, would-be hero stood up, pulled the knife out of his chest and staggered for a moment before falling to the ground beside Rusty with a thud.

Damon assumed his position on top of Sonja once more. She could almost taste the spoiled remains of the ham sandwich he had eaten for lunch on the air escaping through his broken teeth. He caressed her head, drawing closer to his target. Just as their lips neared the resolution of fear and lust, the sound of a gunshot startled Sonja.

She looked at herself, over to Rusty, and back to Damon. She searched for the shot, for where it came from. Damon winced and slumped to his side directly to her left. She looked over to the door frame to see a well-shined shoe covered by pinstriped pants.

"That is not how you treat house guests, Damon," Winters said, a smoking pistol in hand, still pointed at his disobedient grunt.

"You shot me," howled Damon in pain.

"And next time you decide to disobey me, I will not aim for your shoulder," said Winters in a calm, matter-of-fact tone.

"Yes... sir," Damon answered, clutching his dangling arm and walking out of the room.

Winters snapped his fingers and a dozen men entered the room, scurrying to fix the situation. Two men knelt down, picking up Rusty and placing him on a cot another man dragged into the room. Two more rushed over to Sonja, helping her into an upright position. The rest of the men took the body of their fallen comrade out of the room.

"It's so hard to keep a bad dog on a leash," sighed Winters. "Please accept my apologies for his rude behavior."

Sonja just stared and blinked as the well-dressed man attempted to fix the situation as one would a deal gone wrong. He untied her and then presented her a bowl of warm water with a sponge to treat their bruises.

"As you can imagine, we have all been under stressful conditions," Winters said, motioning Sonja over to her unconscious friend.

She snatched the sponge out of the bowl of water, placing it on Rusty's head. She looked Rusty over, checking for blood. She found none, but his shirt was torn and riddled with scuff marks. She gingerly placed her hand on his stomach.

"He could have internal injuries," she quipped. "When Jack returns, he is going to be furious."

Her gaze never left Winters for more than a few seconds.

"I highly doubt there was any permanent damage," retorted Winters, fixing his sleeves, ambling towards the door. "And, in any case, I believe we can both agree Damon was sufficiently punished."

The sound of ceramic breaking echoed throughout the room. Winters raised his left arm beside his face, blocking material from spraying in his direction. He turned on his heels and dashed back to the fiery woman.

"Do not mistake my kindness for weakness," he

said, squeezing her jaw bone. "That is a mistake you would be wise to avoid."

His hand no sooner left her face than he stormed out of the room. The loud bang of the guards slamming the door shut startled Sonja.

"Ugh," grumbled the tiny hero. "Can't you people keep it down around here while a guy takes a nap?"

"You stupid, stupid man," Sonja tried to hide her joy. "You could've gotten yourself killed."

"I couldn't very well let you have all the fun, lassie," wheezed Rusty as he sat up. "Besides, if I hadn't of done that, I wouldn't have this."

Rusty held up a small pocket watch attached to a broken elastic band.

"Wait. How did you," she stammered.

"Thief," he winked while pointing to himself with a grin.

CHAPTER FIFTEEN

Nancy Winters looked like a lengthy purple caterpillar, all snuggled in her slumbering attire, Jack thought. Her dirty blond hair came halfway down her shoulders and smelled of strawberry jam. Nancy's captors had done well not to injure her, save for a few marks around her ankles and wrists from the bindings holding her down. She was a skinny girl with curves in the right places, but to Jack she felt as heavy as an ox, lifting her dead weight to her feet.

Caleb stood watch at the door, peeking around for any sign of movement. The hallway seemed clear. Their friend was still out cold in the room down the hall and there was no sign of additional guards. He signaled for Jack to bring the girl forward.

Jack led Nancy toward the door, her arm draped loosely around his neck like a mink. As the approached the wooden entrance to the pink paradise, Caleb reached for her waist. He was too short to take much weight off Jack, but he was able to help guide her forward.

She began mumbling in her sleep; the drugs were beginning to wear off. Her incoherent ramblings about unicorns, butterflies and sparkles were strange and amusing but increased their likelihood of getting caught.

Jack tried hushing the sleeping beauty, to no avail. He hadn't considered taking an unconscious woman out the way they came in. He hoped she would come to by the time they reached the roof.

He steered Nancy toward the stairwell; Caleb ran ahead. Just as he opened the door two men stepped into view, coming up from the floor below.

"Hey!" one of the startled men exclaimed, reaching for his holstered weapon. "Who are you?"

Caleb slammed the door, flipped the lock and stood in front of it, with his back to the frame.

"Not that way," he said, his arms stretched out wide against the door. "Other way. Other way."

He scampered to Nancy, picking up her legs. Jack hoisted her under the arms and the two began running for the roof, carrying the woman between them. They slipped through the door just as the men forced their way through the locked stairwell door. Caleb locked the roof access door and then the final outer door as they navigated their way to the rooftop.

They carried Nancy to the edge of the building and set her down on the warm cobble top. Jack peered out over the edge. Cars were streaming in from every side street. Jack knew the alarm had gone out.

"So much for the easy way," Jack said, untying the rope from his lassoed pipe.

"What do we do now?" asked Caleb. From the view above, he saw no less than two dozen men storm into the building with guns drawn. "I don't think they're happy we stole their Princess Peach."

"Get up on the ledge," commanded Jack.

"What?" yelped Caleb. "Are you insane?"

"Get on the ledge," Jack repeated himself louder.

Caleb reluctantly climbed on top of the ledge, facing Jack, as he lifted Nancy up, leaning her on the shorter stout man. Jack tied the rope around Caleb's waist then made another tight loop around Nancy.

"Where am I?" a soft voice inquired. Nancy blinked a few times, gathering her bearings.

"Oh, you're going to wish you had slept through this part," Jack said as he finished tying the remainder of the rope around himself. "Caleb, on three."

"One," barked Jack.

Nancy's eyes came into focus, seeing the street below.

"No," she cried, flailing her arms around. "No! No! No!"

"Two," continued Jack.

The door to the roof burst open and off its hinges, flying a few feet before grinding to a stop. Caleb, Nancy and Jack all look to back at the men rushing toward through the portal of bad guys.

Nancy's eyes widened. She flung her arms around Caleb, clutching him close like a new doll on Christmas morning.

"Three," they all yelled together.

Jack pushed off of the roof as Caleb dove backwards, yanking the trio off the enemy-swarmed roof. The rope jolted against its tie-down, struggling to hold their combined weight. They flew down a few feet before the rope caught on itself, springing them across the gap. Jack extended his legs sideways. Caleb covered Nancy's head as best he could. She screamed, hugging Caleb in a vise grip of legs and arms, as she held on for dear life. The group spun sideways, aiming directly for the window in front of them.

A thousand tiny dings echoed in their ears as a cascading waterfall of shattered glass showered around them, everything seeming to happen all at once.

The trio flew through the window of an abandoned law firm, just as the rope snapped. Caleb landed the hardest, cutting his arms and shoulders on the broken glass. He had left himself vulnerable to shield Nancy from so much as a hang-nail.

Jack squinted, blinking repeatedly to bring the world into focus. Jack reached for a large piece of broken glass and used it to free them from their escape apparatus, slicing through knots.

His leather glove tore as he pressed the sharp edges of the glass into the rope. He sawed at their binds until each broke in turn. Jack dropped his bloodied instrument to the ground after the last thread was cut.

The trio scrambled to their feet.

Caleb looked back peeking around the broken window frame towards the roof where they had just taken an enormous leap of faith. The men standing on the ledge looked just as unhappy as they did shocked. One barked, pointing to their location as the others scurried away.

"I don't know whether to thank you or slap you," Nancy said, brushing the broken glass from her hair.

"Don't thank us yet," responded Jack.

He tore off a piece of her gown to use as a wrap for his hand then headed down the dusty road of cubicles in search of the way out. The dust and debris from the crash left the foul taste in his mouth - as if a cloying paste of peanut butter and sawdust were covering it.

A loud ringing in his ears distracted him from his task. Jack considered that he might be suffering from a concussion, but there wasn't time for that; any permanent brain damage would have to wait.

Down the row of unending desks, beside a long-dried-out fern, was a cracked exit sign. Jack motioned for Caleb and pushed the door open looking for the men to be hot on their trail.

There was no one in sight. There wasn't even a sound of a mouse, let alone two dozen angry goons stomping toward them.

They cautiously made their way down the stairs.

On the bottom floor, the stairwell door was ajar. Jack peered around the corner. There, standing in front of the man they had tied up, was a medium-sized man with an emerald cane. He was another dapper man, wearing a dark forest green suit. Jack wondered just how many men in finely tailored, unique suits, could possibly be wandering around town.

The man moved his cane to his other hand,

unscrewing the head from the body. He pulled one part away from the other to reveal a long, sharp blade. He waved it about for a minute then sheathed it once more.

Caleb came up from behind Jack to report the back entrance and his jeep were swarming with bad guys. Jack looked over at Nancy, who was shivering; the silent tears streaming down her face made his gut sink.

"Alright," he yelled out. "We're in here. Don't shoot. I'm unarmed."

The man in the suit walked into the lobby with his head man at his side. Dozens of goons flooded past him with hand guns pointed at Jack. The trio limped out with their hands in the air and their heads hung in defeat.

"Mr. Finder, I presume," said the man with the cane. "You've gone to an awful lot of trouble, and made me go to an awful lot of trouble, to keep you from taking my precious friend away from us. Now, why would you go and do a thing like that?"

"Who cares?" huffed the man Jack had knocked out cold not long ago. His arms crossed, reaching to the holsters on either side of his chest. He pulled out both weapons, aimed them at Jack and then pulled the triggers, sending one bullet flying past Jack's left cheek, another piercing Nancy's pajamas, missing her ankle by millimeters. Seconds later the emerald cane clanged as it hit the floor. The shooter gasped. He looked down to see the steel head firmly planted in the side of his chest. The man in the green suit yanked the thin blade back out from the man's chest, kicked the case up off the floor and shoved the instrument back into its container.

"Now, as I was saying," he continued, as his underling fell to the ground. "I am Mr. Green. She is my prisoner. And you are trespassing."

CHAPTER SIXTEEN

Mr. Green's top floor office was on the opposite side of the building from where Nancy had been held. It looked more like a psychiatrist's place of business than a gangster's hideout. Ferns and other office plants were dotted around the room. There was a large brown couch in the middle, facing a smaller black leather chair with a quaint glass coffee table between the two. At the far end of the room was an old oak desk, with diplomas displayed on the wall behind it. The only light in the room came shining through Venetian blinds, pointed directly toward the well-padded office chair, which held an innocent-looking man who had just murdered his own lackey.

Jack wasn't pleased to be back in the same building again. He couldn't help but think how much easier it was to get into the building then out of it.

"You have to understand the situation," explained Jack with a soft and rational tone. "Nancy is the only way I'm going to get my friends back. If you let me take her to Winters, I'm sure something can be worked out between the two of you."

Green tapped a pencil on the oak desk in a smooth, predictable rhythm. He stared suspiciously at the trio. After a moment or two of thought, he reached into his desk drawer, pulling out a rolled up piece of paper. He unfurled the paper, exposing a map of the town, sectioned off into territories. There was a large red X crossed out through the area containing the Star Lake Club. Two other areas were marked, one with a blue circle and one with red.

"This map signifies the territories of this area," began Green, in the same way someone began a university lecture. "We are currently sitting in the blue area, my area. The red belongs to your employer. And the X was, up until yesterday, controlled by a man named Vincent. Winters has been stepping up the pressure on local businesses, taking them over one by one, under the guise of protection. I simply cannot stand by and allow him to go on pushing me out of my own town."

"I'm not his employee," Jack said, pounding his fist on the table. "I already told you. He has our friends."

He rolled the map back up stuffing it into the drawer from which it came. "Regardless, if he ever wants to see his daughter again, he will comply with my demands and pull his men back."

Green poured himself a glass of aged whiskey from a fine-crystal decanter. It tasted like fire sent directly from heaven as it sloshed down to his stomach. He loved the flavor and the warmth whiskey gave a man. He lifted an empty glass and tipped it toward the two men sitting in the interview chairs directly in front of his desk.

Caleb shook his head. Jack nodded.

"Good man," responded an enthusiastic Green. "You can always tell the measure of a man by what he drinks."

Green turned his back to his guests, poured a generous helping and then handed Jack the glass on his way to perch on the edge of the desk.

"Here's what I can do for you, gentlemen," Green stated in his best car salesman imitation. "I'll let you take Nancy with you and return her to Winters, but on one condition. My men and I will follow you to the exact location of his hideout. Once you have safely rescued your friends, we will handle our business."

Jack stood up. Green clasped his emerald beauty, tapping his fingers as if playing a bugle along the end. The men standing by the door each took one step forward, placing their hands inside their respective jackets. Jack turned away from the desk, striding to the middle of the room, around the coffee table and back.

Green waved his hand downward. The slick gun men resumed their relaxed guarded positions.

"Deal," said Jack.

"What?" Caleb shrieked as he flew off his chair into Jack's path. "You can't be serious.? He will slaughter every last one of Winters' crew. All of those deaths will be on our shoulders."

"They have Rusty and Sonja, Caleb. What else am I supposed to do?"

"Not this. Jack Breeder doesn't get people killed, he saves them."

"And that's exactly what I'm doing," responded

Jack, pushing Caleb out of the way. "You have a deal, Mr. Green."

"Excellent," Green cheered, hopping off the edge of the desk and motioning toward the men who scampered out of the room. "I'm always delighted to work with rational individuals."

He placed his cane on the desk as he moved to fill more glasses of heavenly liquid fire. Green limped past Caleb with a drink in each hand. He extended one out towards Jack. They clinked glasses in a toast of universal understanding.

Jack threw back his shot of whiskey in one huge gulp. He smiled at Green, raising the empty glass in the air. Green laughed, threw back his drink in kind and clanked Jack's glass once more.

The sound of a solid object meeting its target thunked in front of Jack. Green's expression changed from joy to confusion to anger, all within a second. He pivoted on his heels, facing Caleb; Green fell to his knees and followed through to the floor. He landed at Caleb's feet; the short man was clutching an emerald baseball bat.

"Home run," Jack quipped, tipping an imaginary baseball cap to the pint-size slugger.

They rushed over to either side of the entryway. Caleb hid behind the door, the cane still in his clutches. Jack waited up against the door jam. Within a minute, the two greasy gunmen came back through the door with Nancy in bonds.

She led the pack, catching a glimpse of Jack beside the door. Once past his position she dropped to the floor like a sack of potatoes. Before he knew what hit him, the first man was spun around forcefully as Jack captured him in a headlock, using him as a bullet shield. The second man drew his gun.

Caleb let out a grunt kicking the door. It slammed into the second man, causing him to drop his gun. Caleb lifted the cane as high into the air as he could before thrusting it down in the middle of the gunmen's head, knocking him unconscious. Jack tightened his grip on the first gunmen's neck until he went limp. He laid the man, curled into a comfortable position, on top of the other.

"Saving me twice in one day," flirted the pale woman as Jack picked her up off the ground. "A girl could get used to this."

He untied her silk bonds and pushed her toward Caleb. Jack led them outside of the room, closing the door behind them. Just as they entered the hallway, a small patrol group walked by.

Caleb's body became tense; he tightened his grip on the cane.

"You, there," Jack said, calling attention to the misfit gangsters. The squad saw the three of them standing there without a guard and immediately drew their weapons.

"Hey, hey. Whoa," Jack spoke in a hurry. "We're escorting the prisoner to her next location. Get our vehicle ready for us."

The confused men whispered between themselves.

"Says who?" questioned the fat one. "I don't know nothin' about no transfer."

103

"Mr. Green just gave the order," said Jack. "We're going to meet him there later."

"Yeah, I don't think so, pal," said the taller gunman, training his weapon on Caleb.

"Look," rationalized Jack. "Do you honestly believe we would have this if he weren't coming along shortly?"

Caleb held up the emerald-encrusted steel baton.

"No," continued Jack. "He would kill anyone who touched it."

"Huh," said the portly gunman, scratching himself through his pizza stained suit. "I guess you're right. Okay. Let's go, then."

The group of gun toting fools scurried down the stairs to prepare Jack's Jeep. Jack looked over at Caleb, whose face wore a look of surprised confusion and amused bewilderment. They both shrugged their shoulders and headed out.

CHAPTER SEVENTEEN

At the sudden thud of the prison door opening, Sonja startled back to consciousness. She had fallen asleep staring at the minutes ticking by on the stolen watch. Her leg was fast asleep, trapped under her body where she had curled up on the floor next to Rusty's cot. The floor wasn't comfortable, but she felt it was best to let Rusty recover from the fight with Damon on the cot. Although she was cold and damp, Sonja knew it was better to rest when and where she could.

Her attention turned to the men streaming into the room. Three men entered empty-handed, heading straight for the leftover chairs and Rusty's cold, blood-tinged washbasin. Each took a specific object in hand before turning for the exit. Another four men brought in a card table, two cushioned chairs and a space heater.

Sonja shook Rusty awake. She wanted a witness for the amazing sight. He sat straight up on the cot, rubbing his eyes and smacking his lips. He rolled off the edge, walked over and sat in the chair with his arms folded on the table. His head lowered onto his arms, as if to catch a few more winks.

His head popped up wide-eyed and bushytailed. "What the--"

More men entered empty-handed and headed straight for the cot Rusty had vacated seconds before. Two of them folded up the blankets and then removed the cot. Meanwhile, others brought in fresh food for the table. Pancakes stacked abundantly, fresh squeezed orange juice, fruit, butter and all the trimmings, even warm maple syrup.

Rusty's eyes bulged at the feast. He turned to Sonja with the same expression one might have after seeing a donkey juggling chainsaws. His stomach released a noise that could only have been a distress call from a submerged submarine, or a sign of significant hunger. Sonja sat with her legs bent in front of her, elbows firmly planted on her knees holding her head in place, watching the worker bees run by.

Next, Winters entered the room as the last of the servants left. Rusty didn't notice the well-dressed man joining them. He was busy filling his plate with pancakes, sausage and any other food item he could reach on the table.

Sonja rose to her feet. She edged closer to the empty chair by Rusty. Winters smiled, motioning for her to sit, pulling her chair back for her to take a seat. She placed her hand on the edge of the chair. As she was just about to sit down, Damon entered the room with a sling cradling his wounded arm, his other operating a toothpick on his front teeth.

She pushed back away from the table. Her right arm extended, backhanding the fork, on its way to the gaping chasm between his lips, out of Rusty's hand. The dining utensil flew through the air, its load spilling everywhere. Rusty chomped down on thin air with his eyes fully closed.

He opened one eye, raising an eyebrow in Sonja's direction

"Oh, that wasn't necessary," chided Winters. "Damon is simply here to apologize. This meager bit of food is our way of making up his rudeness to our beloved guests. I promise you he's here to play nice. Isn't that right, Damon?" inquired Winters with a rhetorical question.

"Yeah. Nice," Damon replied, with a smirk and a wink aimed at Sonja.

Rusty picked up Sonja's fork, stabbing another bounty of delectable goods. The aroma of breakfast foods topped with syrup and melted butter was intoxicating. Her stomach joined Rusty's in signaling it was time to eat.

"This was all Damon's idea. He is the one who pointed out you must be famished," touted Winters.

Sonja slapped the food away from Rusty again as he was about to take another bite. He grumbled, watching the food in the air.

"We are not eating anything that was... his," she underscored, "idea."

Winters snapped his fingers. As if communicating telepathically, more men poured into the room bringing new silverware, cleaning up the floor and presenting a tall pitcher of dark ale, placed directly in front of Rusty. Winters took one of the new utensils, poked a slab of pancake with sausage and devoured the mouthful.

His hand made a fancy swirling gesture in the air and pointed open palmed towards the food.

"Good enough for me," boasted Rusty. He grabbed a new fork, loaded a plate, positioned his shoulder between Sonja and the food, and then began shoveling it into his belly as fast as he could. He chomped and guzzled, pausing only to give Winters a brief thumbs up.

Winters cringed slightly at the sight of pancake crumbs and ale dripping from Rusty's beard. He forced a smile, allowing the short hungry man to go back to filling the Grand Canyon in his lower torso.

Sonja sat down, took up a plate with a small bit of pancake, tiny piece of sausage and a glass of juice. She cut an abysmally small bite. It was delicious, perhaps one of the best breakfast meals she had ever tasted. Everything was cooked to perfection and the juice was so fresh it was as if she were drinking from an orange with a straw, minus the nasty pulp.

"Good. Now that we're all friends again, we can anticipate the return of your hero, Mr. Finder, which shall be soon; then everyone can go on about their daily lives," Winters said as he exited the room. "Enjoy."

Damon followed a few seconds later, leaving a bit of a gap between the two men. He reached for the door and began closing it as he walked out. He turned, bowing a quarter of his height.

"Either that or this was your last meal," snarked Damon, as he finished shutting the door, laughing.

Rusty and Sonja halted their consumption to

look at each other. Neither of them had to say a word. They both knew he was right and if Jack didn't hurry up, the meal really would be their last.

CHAPTER EIGHTEEN

The ride back from Green's hideout was rather tense. Both Jack and Caleb were painfully aware of how close they were cutting it. They had only been given 24 hours to return Nancy; a fact of which she was completely unaware. As far as she knew, they were simply her saviors; men her father had probably paid to come to her aid and rescue her from a bad situation.

Something told Jack it probably wasn't the first time she'd had to be rescued, and it probably wouldn't be the last; neither of which was his concern. What he was concerned about was the well-being of his captured comrades.

By the time the Jeep finally arrived at Winters' inconspicuous hideout, Jack had melted into a panic. He parked the Jeep hurriedly and hopped out. Nancy scooted to the edge of the back seat, where she paused to tell Caleb about the first time she had seen the building. Jack reached into the vehicle, placing one hand firmly under each of her arms, and lifted her up and out of the Jeep.

She squealed with delight, raising one foot up off the ground after landing, pulling a piece of her hair with two fingers of her left hand. She loved the smell of a man's sweat. Something about Jack was particularly fascinating to Nancy's nostrils.

Caleb rolled his eyes, exiting the vehicle himself with a huff. Much to their surprise, no armed guards or men in overpriced suits greeted them at the door. The place seemed empty and that didn't sit well with Jack. There was no traffic. There were no lights in any of the windows around the place. It was as if they had entered another dimension, where it was only them and the building.

Jack was still aware of the time. He was unable to give into his instinctive caution. The setting wasn't right and his gut was screaming at him to turn back, but there was nothing he could do. Time was almost up and he had lives to save.

Once they moved into the belly of the building, the well-armed men in good-looking suits began to appear. They weren't as prevalent as they had been the last time the duo had traversed the halls of the hideout, but they were definitely there.

At last they came upon the area where security clearance was necessary. Damon was leaning over the front desk where a tall, busty brunette was stationed behind a telephone and a notepad. She was gushing. She let her finger trail down his arm, batting the eyelashes in front of her ice-blue eyes.

"So, I had to take down a dozen of them all by myself before this lucky little punk got off a shot. I made him regret that when I ripped off his arm and started beating him with it," peacocked Damon.

"Ohhh," cooed the brunette. "I love a man who can take care of himself," she said, leaning over toward him even more.

Jack raised an eyebrow at Caleb, who was making gagging gestures. Nancy squirmed, looking anywhere in the room except at the spectacle in front of them. Jack noticed even a few of the guards by the door were grinning and grimacing, holding in laugher at the ridiculous conversation. Jack could nearly taste the combination of testosterone, alcohol and steroids in the air.

"Ahem," one of the guards cleared his throat to attract Damon's attention.

Damon turned his head immediately locking eyes with Jack. The brunette glared at Nancy, who smiled in return.

"Well, look who came back," snarled Damon as he walked up to the group. "Sorry to tell you, but you're a little late, Finder. Your friends are gone, but don't worry. I took real good care of them."

Jack shoved Damon out of the way, sprinting for the steel door with Caleb close behind. Jack reared back his right fist, landing it straight across the jaw of the sentinel on the right. Caleb leapt at the man on the left side of the door. The guard reacted by catching the shorter man in midair, allowing Caleb to head-butt the guy with all of this might. Both guards slid to the floor. Jack stepped over them and entered the room.

"Sonja!" He yelled.

"Rusty!" Caleb barked.

Damon doubled over, slapping his knee. He was laughing so hard tears were streaming from his eyes. He walked toward the room, hitting the wall with his open hand and pointing at the two men on

112

their knees in front of the empty breakfast table.

"Ah haha," chirped the muscle-bound man. "I'm just messing with ya. We moved them down to the garage bay. You should've seen the expressions on your faces!"

Jack balled his fists; rage replaced the abject sorrow he had suddenly felt tearing through his soul. He stood, one leg off the ground enough to allow him to push off and take a swing from a half kneeling position. His knuckles landed in Damon's rigid stomach, stifling his laughter. He forced Damon back a few feet before the massive man stopped the momentum by tossing Jack onto the hard marble floor.

Caleb rushed to Jack's aid, kicking Damon in the knee. The kick wasn't enough to affect the steroid-infused psychopath, as Caleb noticed, being hoisted a few feet into the air by the back of his collar.

"Alright, fellas," Damon said, as if breaking up the schoolyard fight. "Let's go. I'd enjoy playing with you all day, but Mr. Winters will want to see you, now."

He tossed Caleb over by Nancy, landing him on his feet after a few quick moves. Jack pushed himself up off the ground knocking away Damon's hand. Nancy stood, mortified, shaking her head from one side to the other. Damon walked by the desk with his prey leaning backwards on it.

"I'll see you later," Damon said to the brunette who was fawning all over him to the point of dry-humping his leg in front of everyone.

The group trudged down the endless corridors of the hideaway, gathering minions who followed Damon like rats after the Pied Piper. They were pushed and shoved all the way to their destination. A stack of tires twice the height of Jack acted as pillars, holding up the gateway to the meeting place.

The garage was an impressive sight. Cars lined both sides of a thousand square foot room with three garage door openings. The ceiling was three stories high, with large glass bay windows and an old car chassis hanging from the rafters. There were men who appeared to be mechanics, greased up, working on cars, while others lined up for a convoy.

Jack saw Winters standing around a group of men, telling a story. The group seemed to be enjoying the words emanating from the charismatic boss man. As they approached, Winters moved just enough to give Jack a glimpse of Sonja. She was sitting comfortably on a stack of tires, with Rusty tinkering on an engine block beside her.

One of the minions tapped Winters on the shoulder, pointing to the nearing entourage. He turned, seeing Jack and Caleb front and center winged on either side by Nancy and Damon. His expression lit up at seeing Nancy safe and sound. She waved, trotting over to her father. Caleb walked by them both, coming up behind Rusty, firmly placing his foot on Rusty's ass before giving it a slight shove. Rusty's head hit the metal. He climbed back out of the block, cursing, ready to fight the offender. Caleb just stood smiling as his brother realized who had given him the shove.

Jack walked toward Sonja with purpose, brushing by Winters, ignoring the stout brothers' horseplay. He stopped directly in front of Sonja, who rose to greet him. She smiled wider and felt more cheerful than she ever had to see anyone in her entire life. He reached out, sliding his hand up from her hand, along her arm and up to her face. She cocked her head to the side pushing into his hand. She allowed him to pull her face toward his and closed her eyes as their lips followed the magnetic path to one another's.

"Daddy!" Nancy exclaimed at the top of her lungs, reaching out and grabbing Jack's shoulder, pulling him away from Sonja just as their lips were about to meet. "This man saved me twice in one day. Thank you so much for sending him."

"Only the best for my daughter," Winters responded with delight. "Now, why don't you run back upstairs and get freshened up? Go to the kitchen and get the staff started on our feast. We must thank our most generous new friends for reuniting us."

"Of course, Daddy," she squealed again, grating Jack's nerves.

Nancy leaned in, hugging her hero as close as she could, glaring at Sonja. "And thank you, too, Mr. Jack," she said pulling her head back, planting a kiss firmly on his cheek, close to the corner of his lips.

Sonja stepped forward, catching the younger woman's eye. "Okay, I'll see you soon," Nancy cheered, bouncing off the way they came. Sonja clenched her fist, muttering to herself. Rusty reached up and patted her on the back.

"Now," Winters restarted, redirecting the conversation. "We will feast together tonight, and you, my dear boy, shall be compensated for all of your troubles. I won't hear otherwise. I owe you quite a debt of gratitude. All of you."

"But before we can begin, I must go and ensure this never happens again."

"Damon!" Winters yelled, snapping his fingers.

"Let's go, boys," yelled Damon, as he rushed to one of the waiting cars. All the cars that had been lined up in front of the closed doors filled with suits carrying guns. Damon jumped in the shotgun position of the car furthest back. It was lined with gold around the trim. The doors looked to be reinforced with thick glass panes.

"I assure you everything will be sorted out momentarily and then I will get to the pressing issue of your recompense," a more serious Winters announced to the four of them. "Head on inside with Nancy until I return."

Jack attempted to decline, but Winters was already marching off to the sturdiest car. Jack sighed, placing his left arm around Sonja and right hand behind Rusty's back, ushering them back to the place they called prison not that long ago.

It was sure to be a slaughter, but that wasn't Jack's business and his job was done. He knew the way the crime bosses worked. Kidnapping Winters' daughter was an act of war. A war Winters was going to win. And if Winters wanted to attempt to make the situation right, Jack wasn't going to turn down a payday after everything they had gone through.

"Let's go. Let's go," Damon yipped and hollered, riling up the men in the cars, who quickly joined in with a battle cry of joyful noise.

One of the grease monkeys ran over to the door, pushing the giant green button activating the motors above the roof. The tall garage doors began opening. The drivers began revving their cars' engines. The setting sun shone through under the door, casting its last bit of energy for the day on the fleet of well-dressed gunmen being released like a pack of vicious attack dogs.

Jack turned back to watch them leave. The tired group stood by the garage entrance to the hideout. Suddenly, his eyes caught shadows being cast from outside the doors. He quickly realized it wasn't one, two, or three--but dozens of shadows were appearing. Jack tried to yell to Winters. He was drowned out by the sound of the battle cries emanating from the cars.

The doors came up revealing a dozen or more similar cars placed in a semicircle outside of the garage bay. Jack could see one dark green suit in the middle of all the others, hidden behind the opposing army of vehicles. Dozens of men were stationed at every strategic angle outside the garage, pointing their weapons with deadly intent.

CHAPTER NINETEEN

Caleb looked down at the green cane and then back up at Jack as the sound of gunfire washed over them like a tsunami. Jack tried to yell out, but it was too late.

For Jack, time slowed down. Outside the building, every pop from every gun lit up with a flash as bullets left their starting points on their journey to destroy human life. Jack was no stranger to death. He wasn't afraid to get his hands dirty. His hands had seen the stain of blood before, but the imagery in front of them burned a permanent residence in his brain. The ambush was unlike anything he, let alone the rest of the group, had ever seen.

Pop. Pop. Pop. Aimless and careless, the gangsters sprayed death like an aerosol can. Jack could see the expressions of joy and satisfaction on the faces of those behind the mechanisms. Random, zigzag patterns of bullets laced the air, decimating every visible target.

The front car of each procession took the brunt of the damage. Metal stripped off of metal, one piece at a time, exposing the undercarriages and innards of each vehicle. When the shielding was removed, the bullets passed through unhindered, slamming into the bodies of the unsuspecting men within-- a few of whom had been caught mid-celebration.

One man fell down with his arms still raised. Another dropped face first onto a cleaning rag stained with grease; he was no criminal, just a mechanic doing his job fixing cars. Cars that had been turned into fire bombs and metallic coffins.

Death continued to rain from Green's storm, but at a certain point Jack shut off. He was unable to process the scene. Instead, he threw out his arms, pushing everyone backward into the door frame, where they were shielded, to some degree, by the stacks of tires on other side of the door. The fireworks weren't aimed in their direction and the few shots that did stray their way were absorbed by the rubber towers.

In less than a minute, Green's army had mowed down Winters' entire crew.

Time sped up again for Jack. Indistinct yelling evolved into roaring orders to cease fire, coming from the commander in green.

A cloudy mixture of gunfire, metal shavings and smoke filled the air. Jack could taste the blackness of death hanging all about them, putrid and stomach turning. The unmistakable smell of hot metal permeated the room filling the void of unpleasant noise with unpleasant odor.

Not more than 100 yards away was the gold-lined car. Its thickened glass windows had held unshattered. The body of the vehicle was dented all along the front and right hand side. Jack realized that Winters may have survived the fire-fight, being in a superior vehicle compared to all the rest. Before his eyes, light emanated from inside the vehicle: two distinct flashes, followed by a brief pause and then another three flashes.

Green's men were already inundating the room, pouring in like cockroaches hunting a morsel of honey. Jack wanted to move to the vehicle, but doing so would mean giving away their position and doom his group to being slaughtered in the same way the well-tailored suits had just been.

A minute later the armored car was surrounded by goons, all pointing their weapons at the invincible automobile. They yelled for the inhabitants to exit the vehicle. Jack knew it was the end for the man who had kidnapped his friends, but felt no sense of satisfaction. If anything, he felt guilt. He and Caleb had led Green straight to Winters, wrapped him in a pretty little bow and handed him over. All without realizing it.

Winters had done a horrible thing for all the right reasons. Jack considered how he might do the same thing if his daughter, should he ever have one, ended-up kidnapped, forcing his back against the wall.

His rationalization of the attack before him was cut short by the armored car's door opening. He had expected the back door to open and Winters to step out, arms reaching to the sky, only to be sliced apart by the dozen itchy triggers pointing in his direction. Yet it was not the back door that opened.

The front passenger door opened with a kick from the inside. The lock had been jammed by a bullet that had pierced the mechanism inside. Once open, a bloodied Damon rose from the smoldering vehicle with a handgun in one hand. There was too much blood over Damon's face for him to still be conscious.

The gunmen lowered their pieces.

Damon climbed out as the man in the dark green suit entered Jack's line of vision. He pushed one man aside, walking right up to Damon, raising his replacement cane in the air.

And then it hit Jack square in the gut. Green pumped the cane into the air, hollering a cheer, extending his other hand to Damon. The blood-soaked brute tossed the gun down, wiped the blood off the side of his face, reaching down to shake. The men embraced as the group cheered.

Jack realized the flashes had been from Damon's gun. The dog had betrayed the hand that fed him. They hadn't been followed after all. The suspiciously deserted buildings and the horrible gut instinct Jack had ignored suddenly made sense. Green knew where Winters was thanks to his second in command turning on the boss. It was all a set up.

Damon had killed two of the three bosses; the Syndicate would blame Jack for starting the war, and end his career. Green would be left to run the town unopposed.

Jack was startled by glass shattering on the ground behind them, followed by a desperate scream. He turned to see Nancy standing at the doorway, feet planted on the ground surrounded by a pool of lemonade with glass shards sprinkled here and there. She fell forward into Jack's arms.

The group of gun toting men had also been alerted to their presence by the scream. Green, Damon and their peers were staring directly at the group of bystanders from across the bay.

"Get them!" commanded Damon, sending the minions running for the door. Jack threw Nancy over his shoulder in his well-practiced fireman's lift and followed Sonja, who was already sprinting ahead. Rusty and Caleb each grabbed a tire from the lower end of the stack, pulling with everything they had, sending the towers of rubber crashing down, forming a crisscrossed barrier.

A bullet whizzed by Caleb, drilling into the wall behind them, while another buried itself in a falling piece of rubber half a foot in front of Rusty. The pair looked at each other and hightailed it down the hall after Jack.

Sonja plowed full-steam ahead in her search for the end of the corridors. The marble maze seemed to stretch out in endless miles of walls in front of her. Jack had caught up and the two brothers followed close behind.

Immediately in front of her, to the left, a man appeared with his weapon drawn. She raised her left, leg forcefully jamming her shoe between his arms and dislodging the weapon as her foot impacted under his chin. He fell to the ground, as did his gun, which discharged harmlessly into the wall.

Three more men ran into the hall from various

rooms, alerted by the shot. The first to arrive met Sonja's best right hook, square in his left eye. The next arrived as the first slammed face first into the drywall. Sonja fell to her knees, sliding nearly a foot. She crashed her shoulder to the ground, tumbling end over end, her full revolution ending on her back with both legs locked together, cramming both feet into the groin of the second man. Her heart raced. A bullet grazed her cheek as she sat up. She eyed the man who had fired the shot for only the second before hearing another pop from behind.

Jack knelt down, taking the pistol from the first assailant, and fired off a shot from the hip. The bullet struck the third man in the chest, causing him to fall backwards and through a table at the end of the hall.

Sonja pushed off the ground, continuing to run ahead.

The halls were empty as far as they could see. Jack assumed the men had been scouts, combing the building for Winters' men. At the end of another hallway, adjacent to the one with the broken table and a dead man, were the doors Jack and Caleb had entered through when they had first arrived.

The Jeep was still waiting outside. Neither camp of men had had the foresight to move the vehicle, but that suited Jack just fine. Jack laid Nancy down on the floor in the back before climbing into the driver's seat. Sonja hopped in the passenger side. The brothers hurried to the getaway vehicle, with Rusty jumping in the back and nearly stepping on

Nancy's head.

Caleb stopped, bent over hands-on his knees outside of the vehicle.

"Come on, Caleb! We need to go!" Sonja urged.

"I'm coming," responded Caleb, one word at a time, heavy breaths in between.

"Caleb?" Sonja said with a question in her voice. By the time the words had left her lips, Caleb had hit the sidewalk like a felled tree. She leapt from her seat to aid the man on the ground. She rolled him over on his back to check his breathing. Her hand retracted from his side at the feel of lukewarm liquid. Sonja looked down to see red dripping from the fingertips.

"Jack!" She screamed, lifting her little buddy off the ground.

Jack was backing up the vehicle, preparing to speed away when she screamed. His eyes widened when he realized what she was doing. As Sonja brought Caleb to the vehicle his arms dangled backward, still clutching his prized emerald cane. She set him in the back with his brother and climbed into the passenger seat on her knees facing the back of the vehicle.

Rusty yelled for his brother, to no avail. He reached down, ripping the sleeve off the left arm of the unconscious girl on the floor to use as a bandage. Pressing the cloth against the wound, Rusty continued to plead with Caleb to respond.

Up above them, at the doorway of the building, Green's men began to appear, pointing toward the Jeep. Jack slammed the gear shift into reverse, peeling backwards then smoking the tires as he threw the Jeep into drive. The slight dust cloud the maneuver kicked up gave them just enough cover to get away without further injury, but the damage had already been done.

CHAPTER TWENTY

The drive was silent, except for the sobbing coming from the back seat. Sonja spun around, with her ass firmly planted in the seat. Jack stared blankly at the road in front of them. It was night and the moon was shining brightly, but even with as many stars as there were in the sky, it seemed an empty place to Jack.

There were other cars on the street. Headlights shone in through the windshield as they passed by. Even the windows of shops that hadn't yet closed were still lit, people browsing inside. Signs of life were all around them and yet he felt alone.

The nearest clinic was still minutes away. Jack drove as fast as the Jeep allowed, breezing by everything in their path.

He could see Rusty in the rear-view mirror, cradling his brother, rocking back and forth in the backseat. Caleb's face had lost its color. As the blood drained from his body, so did the color from his rosy cheeks. Death was pulling his life force away and there was nothing they could do about it.

Charway Free Medical Care was a twelve-bed clinic that low income and homeless people used in emergency situations. They were staffed 24 hours a day, running a skeleton crew at night. No one ever stayed unless it was serious and the county hospital wouldn't take them. It was located in a rundown part of town, where even the cops didn't rove. The paint on the outside of the building was peeling and the sign in front of the place only lit up the words "Free Med," but that was enough to get the point across for those that needed their services.

When they finally arrived at the clinic, Jack noticed that the doors were shut. The lights were on, but no one was going in or out. He stopped the vehicle at the end of the 50 foot circular driveway. Rusty urged him to keep going, yelling, "He's dying!" through brotherly tears. Jack couldn't shake the feeling that something just wasn't right.

The air smelled of burnt rubber and cleaning fluid. The medical-grade stuff was excellent for killing germs, but toxic enough to remove skin if the person wielding the chemicals wasn't smart enough to use protection. It was so bad Jack could practically taste chlorine.

Fearing for Caleb's life, Jack chose to ignore his gut feeling; he continued up the driveway and parked in front of the building. Jack slammed on the horn for someone to run outside and help them. He hit the horn again and again. No one came.

Sonja unbuckled her seatbelt. She made to climb out but Jack grabbed her by the shoulder and pushed her back down into the seat. His eyes never looked over in her direction, still panning the area for danger. She knocked his hand away, seeing no one around them.

As she rose up from her seat again, high beams from a vehicle hidden in the bushes in front of them roared to life. Two more lit up behind them and another four on either side of the two at the back.

Jack threw the Jeep into gear. His foot crushing the pedal. The force threw Sonja back into her seat as he rolled the steering wheel hard to the left. The sturdy old vehicle rocked as they climbed over the dying grass and mounded dirt surrounding the half lit up sign, lurched over the sidewalk and landed, wheels-down, facing the wrong way on the two lane street.

The horn of a truck heading straight for them blared. Jack swerved right and the truck swerved left, the vehicles missing each other by inches, sending the truck careening into one of the vehicles giving chase. He started veering down hard turns in an attempt to lose their pursuers, but two cars were still hot on their trail.

Jack reached down to the floor, grabbing some metal tools in his fist. He handed Sonja a crowbar, wrench and other random tools. She turned around in her seat with one arm cradling the goods and the arm holding the biggest tool of the bunch. She started launching one after another over Rusty's head and in the direction of the chasing cars.

The crowbar missed, striking the ground and flying off to the side of the road. She tossed a pair of pliers and a few screwdrivers, which all met the pavement too. Her last tool was the monkey wrench Jack used to work on the engine block. It was a top-heavy instrument with scratches and dents from work it had performed over the years, yet it still shone like new, thanks to Jack's meticulous care of the things he owned.

She took careful aim and tossed the wrench sideways, as hard as she could. The lead vehicle behind them slammed on its brakes as its windshield shattered under the force of the wrench plunging through the glass. The vehicle in the rear clipped the back right side of the stopped vehicle, sending the left side of the automobile into midair. It drove on two wheels in a hard curve to the right, directly into a ditch that promptly swallowed it whole.

Jack and Rusty cheered. She smiled, sliding back down into the seat. The thrill of the momentary victory faded quickly as the gravity of the situation set in. The failed ambush had tipped Green's hand. Jack knew they would be looking for them at their homes, hospitals, clinics and friend's houses. He felt it was a bad idea to even stop by a pharmacy. Caleb was still in the backseat and still very much on his way to the big thief guild in the sky.

There was only one place in town Jack could guarantee Green wouldn't go. And it was also the one place in town no one in the car would be invited, particularly the members in the backseat.

He stole another glance in the rear view mirror, catching Rusty's eye. Their gazes met, locking onto one another. He frowned at Rusty, who in turn looked down at his brother and back up at the mirror. Rusty shook his head from side to side, a

129

single tear running down his cheek.

Jack looked away and then to Sonja. He looked in the mirror again and back to the road. Letting out a huge sigh, Jack forced the steering wheel hard left, cutting across traffic and almost rolling the vehicle. There was one hope left, both for their safety and Caleb's life.

CHAPTER TWENTY ONE

The commissioner's mansion was located on the tallest hill at the southern end of town. Locals called it The Tower. The people below could see the lights in the mansion watching over the town from afar. It was quite removed from everything and that was exactly how the owners liked it.

Jack pulled up to the 25 foot steel reinforced gate, positioned at the bottom of the hill leading to The Tower. He reached out the window and pushed the button for the guard to open the gate.

After a few buzzes, a roly-poly old man meandered to the gate. He wore a security uniform with a tool belt around his waist and badge over his heart. The uniform looked to be two sizes too small and ten years too old. The belt was as dingy as the badge and missing all of its tools. His old eyes weren't what they used to be, causing the guard to squint at the Jeep. He moved his left hand up and over his eyes in an attempt to block out some of the light coming from the vehicle's headlights.

"Who are you?" asked the man.

Jack made some muffled responses.

"Who?" asked the man louder, with some confusion.

When he didn't hear a response the guard reached into his pocket pulling out a set of keys twice the size of his hands. He fumbled for the appropriate key, using the wrong key more than twice before finding one that fit. When he finally enabled the gates to open Jack waved the man towards his door.

"Morning, sir," Jack said with confidence. "We're here to see the commissioner. We have a six o'clock meeting."

The man looked down at his watch. He squinted again, moving the watch closer and further attempting to focus. "It's not the morning yet."

"It's almost six and we're going to be late," Jack said, pointing to his bare wrist.

"Oh," the poor old guard scratched his head. "I thought it was just after midnight. You better get going then."

Jack smiled and nodded, applying pressure to the gas pedal.

The Tower was, in all reality, a six bedroom house made from the finest French materials. There were white silk curtains in every window facing out to the town, surrounded by meticulously crafted molding. The roof was rounded to allow the proper acoustics for the harp player they employed on Friday nights to entertain their well-to-do friends.

The commissioner and his wife never accepted anything but the best. Between the two of them, they pulled in quite a sum of money. She was the senior surgeon at the county hospital, making boatloads of cash from every gallbladder removed.

And her husband collected a nice total from what the town paid him in salary and what the criminals paid him on the side.

The lawn dwarfed the whole building with acres of grass, surrounding the house and driveway on all sides. The driveway itself was paved smooth as butter all the way up to the front door, with not a single divot in the road. The path led to a complete circle, encompassing a marble fountain with angels dripping water into a pond. Stairs sat in front of the entryway with thick red wood doors and slats of glass beside and above them.

Jack parked the Jeep in a hurry, with one tire up on the sidewalk. He climbed out, as Sonja who went to the back to assist Rusty. Jack looked down at the floor he noticed Nancy was still there and unconscious, breathing heavily with a snore. What was left of her top, after Rusty tore off pieces of the cloth to stop Caleb's bleeding, rose and fell with the same rhythm of a sleeping baby. He shook his head, stepping over her to take Caleb's body from Rusty.

Jack lowered his head to the short man's chest. He was still breathing, but it was shallow and difficult to hear. Jack met Rusty and Sonja as they climbed up the stairs. Rusty took one at a time with Sonja bounding three in each stride.

She pounded on the door with her left fist, and then slammed the knocker three times, breaking it off the hinge with her right hand. Sonja paused to toss the brass away. Just as her fist cocked back to knock again, an older lady with fair, wrinkled skin answered the door in her full-body sleeping attire.

Sonja wedged her foot in the door, forcing it open more than the crack it was given at first.

"Who are you and what do you want?" inquired the old woman from beneath the nightcap protecting her hair.

"My name is Sonja and my friend has been injured," she said pointing to Jack as he cradled Caleb's body. "We need help."

"I'm sorry, the owners don't allow people into the house this late at night. Go to the free clinic downtown," she said as she attempted to push Sonja's foot out of the door to close it.

"We don't have time for this," roared Rusty pushing Sonja out of the way and slamming his head straight into the door, sending it flying open.

The old woman screamed as Jack marched in behind Rusty. She started hitting Jack, hand over hand on his back, yelling "Get out!"

Sonja peeled her off Jack, leading her to sit in a wooden chair, positioned by a mahogany cabinet in the foyer of the house.

The long circular staircase led to the second floor. There was a table with flowers in the middle of the room with an expensive crystal chandelier hanging high in the ceiling. To the left and right were various rooms used for comfort and entertainment. One door, on the opposite side from the entrance, was a swinging door to some sort of food area, Jack presumed.

He followed Rusty into what appeared to be a game room. There were large leather chairs positioned around the fireplace, just like at home for

Jack but in a much smaller room. Jack's living room barely fit the chairs and rug let alone leather chairs, bookcases, animal trophies on the wall and a regulation size pool table in the middle of the room like that. Jack walked by the pool table and over to the large matted couch covered by an antique, monogrammed afghan.

He laid Caleb down with a gentle touch, arranging his arms as if the small man were slumbering.

"What is the meaning of this?" snarled a tall, dark-skinned man wearing pajama bottoms and a thick cotton robe monogrammed with the same letters as the afghan. He was not a young man, yet he didn't look aged. His chiseled arms and chest showed through the clothing. He was well-built, not like a bodybuilder, but more of a man who had worked in physical environments all of his life. He wore his goatee in a circular fashion around his mouth, the corners of which turned down at the sight of the intruders in his home.

"You!" he bellowed, catching sight of Jack rising away from Caleb.

"Hello, Sergeant Davis. Long time no see." Jack moved over to him. Both men's fists clenched tight, ready for action.

"Honey, what's going on?" said a woman in her mid to late forties as she came around the corner of the door frame.

She was a beautiful woman with smooth cocoa butter skin. She wore a similar bathrobe, only hers was left untied revealing a red midriff free lace top and matching silk pants.

Davis moved over to her, reaching his arm around her shoulders. "What are you doing in my lounge in the middle of the night, Finder?"

"I'm not here to fight," Jack responded, opening his arms, showing his palms face up. "I need your wife's help. My friend has been shot, there are people after us and we have nowhere else to go."

The woman looked concerned, peering around Jack towards the man on the couch.

"No. No way, Finder. I'm not getting mixed up in whatever you're into this time," responded Commissioner Davis in sheer defiance.

"They need my help, Reginald," declared his wife, the surgeon. "I took an oath to help people in need and that's what I'm going to do." She broke free from his grasp and rushed to Caleb's side.

She knelt down on the floor beside the couch, moving the unconscious man's left arm out of the way. Her hands peeled the purple cloth make-shift bandages away from his side. They were drenched in blood to the point of dripping.

"This is bad. This is a really, really bad." The surgeon removed what was left of Caleb's shirt from around the injury, clearing her line of sight. She shook her head, muttering to herself.

Jack leaned over her shoulder, at the ready in case there was anything he could do. The wound was no longer bleeding, but it was much bigger than he expected.

"I need my bag from the other room." She pushed off of the couch, propelling herself up and out of the room.

"You have a whole lot of explaining to do," growled Davis.

"Don't worry, sergeant, you and I will have a nice little chat," Jack quipped, his voice dripping with sarcasm.

"That's commissioner, now, you over-glorified thief."

The men stormed toward one another with violent intent. Sonja sidestepped in between them, holding her arms out on either side.

"There will be plenty of time for this later, boys," she announced in her best motherly tone.

Jack backed off to Caleb's side, while Davis trudged out of the room. His dramatic exit was far less important to Jack when the doctor came back into the room. She had her bag in one hand and fresh warm, damp cloths in the other. Her robe was gone, replaced by a scrub top he figured she had thrown on for the procedure.

She looked at Jack and Rusty, who were standing side-by-side at the lower end of the couch. "This isn't going to be easy. I have no guarantee this will work. He really should be in the hospital."

"It's this or nothing, doctor," Jack answered with trepidation.

She nodded, opened her bag and began.

CHAPTER TWENTY TWO

Nancy sobbed in the corner of the room furthest away from everyone. The deep lounge chair enveloped the young woman. She sat with her knees drawn up to her chest, curled in a ball, resting her head against the back of the matted seat.

Jack sat beside Sonja with his back against the facade of the fireplace. Her head rested on his shoulder while his head rested against the cold, hard bricks. The look of worry on his face and hadn't left since the doctor started her impromptu operation. The smell of burnt oak embers coming from the crackling firewood reminded him of home, providing a much-needed distraction.

His vantage point gave him sight of the entire room, including where Caleb lay unconscious on the couch, with blankets tucked all around him. Jack sipped on a small glass of sweet lemonade the old woman had brought them. It was loaded with sugar, but it quenched his thirst.

He offered some to Rusty but he decided to lie on the floor beneath Caleb instead. For the first time ever, Rusty turned down a drink. Rusty was still as if asleep, but his gaze bore holes in the ceiling above. He shook at times. Yet he was holding together better than Jack imagined he would in the same situation.

"There isn't anything we can do now except wait," the doctor announced softly to the group. "It's all up to him, now."

Rusty sat up, looking at the doctor. "If anyone is too stubborn to die, it's my brother."

Sonja nodded with a warm smile and nodded at him in agreement.

The doctor walked over to where her husband stared out of the window. It was a bit strange to Jack. She came up behind him and placed her arms around his waist, resting her head against his shoulder. He realized it was often easy to forget people with such power can be as human as the rest of folk.

"No one would ever imagine I would come here," Jack said as he eased Sonja's head off his shoulder.

"Did you ever consider that's because you probably should not have?" huffed Davis.

His wife patted his shoulder.

"You know as well as I do if we hadn't ended up here we would all be in the morgue," argued Jack.

Davis stayed silent, as if biting his tongue. He turned to face Jack. "Well, you're here now. You mind telling me when you're going to leave? Your friend needs to be in the hospital, not lying in my games room. And you're putting my family in danger, being here."

"Can't you send your boys over to Green's place and arrest them?" asked Jack, knowing the answer full well.

The look on Davis' face changed from sheer annoyance to humanistic concern. "The peace between the force and the Syndicate is as thin as a sheet of paper, after all the killing. They've been at each other for weeks. If I make a move like that, and Green ends up winning the war, I'll be out of this town in a moving truck or a box within a week."

Jack let out a sigh as he walked back to Sonja. He stood in front of her, looking into her eyes, reaching for her hand. "Green has already won his war."

After a moment of solitude, Jack broke his stare and refocused on Nancy. He turned and crouched in front of her.

"I know this is very hard for you, but I need your help. Do you know what this war is all about? What started it? What might end it?"

She remained silent, looking right past him into the nothingness in the void beyond.

Jack dropped his head. "Please, Nancy. Help us."

Every conscious member of the group stared in her direction. Nancy began shifting towards the cold steel of Jack's eyes as he looked back up.

Her arms uncrossed. She reached her left hand into the tattered purple top. From a tiny pocket hidden behind the stitching of a pink flower above her right breast, she pulled out a folded note and handed it to Jack.

He unfolded the note which had no more room than to write a short series of numbers.

"I promised I would always keep it with me," said the childlike-woman through her cracking voice. "He said if anything ever happened to him I was supposed to go to his warehouse and use those numbers to unlock the safe. But he said nothing would ever happen, so I shouldn't worry," she interrupted herself, breaking out into a fresh round of sobbing again.

The doctor came over. "There, there. It's okay. Let's go see if we can find you some hot cocoa."

She reached down to take Nancy's hand and put her arm around the young woman's back, lifting her off of the seat and guiding her into the kitchen.

"Green will have men there, Jack," Sonja said, rising up from her seated position near the fire.

Jack nodded. "I know. But we don't have any choice. This must've been what Green was after when he kidnapped Nancy. It was underneath his nose the entire time."

Rusty hopped up from his place near Caleb, using the coffee table as a crutch. The wood groaned under his weight and the front left leg buckled, splitting out from the rest of the table, sending it to the ground with a thud.

"Whoops," blushed Rusty.

Jack put his hand to his forehead, closing his eyes.

"My coffee table!" exclaimed Davis.

"They just don't build them like they used to anymore," snapped Rusty.

Sonja glared at the short man. He smiled back.

A soft shade of red, similar to the luscious red

apples sitting in the basket in the entryway, rushed over Davis. "Get out of my house. Get out!"

"Your friend will be safe here," Davis' wife spoke in a soft, reassuring voice as she leaned against the door frame. "Go. But be careful."

Sonja grabbed both of the guys, leading them out of the house.

CHAPTER TWENTY THREE

Winters' warehouse was twice the size of his hideout, even with the inclusion of the launch pad for automobile warfare. Jack, Sonja and Rusty sat parked a block away from the large gray brick building. It had one entryway in the middle with windows on all three floors. The steep, slanted roof provided excellent coverage against the elements, but it also eliminated the possibility of an entrance from the top. The reinforced steel doors at the front of the building and whatever docking bay was at the back were the only ways Jack could figure to get in.

There was no one in sight. If there were patrols, Jack couldn't see them. He had cased a thousand buildings in his career, but that one was huge. He considered the possibility of people inside. Even with the lack of movement on the outside, there could be an army on the inside and they wouldn't know it.

He decided they would wait until night fell, when it would be easier to slip inside, in case there were any guards watching the outside.

While they waited, Rusty handed out some fruit he had pocketed from the mansion. Jack remarked on how delightful a banana can be when one is starving. They agreed, each devouring their own.

As the shadows elongated, the team dozed behind cover of trees and parked cars along the street. Jack kept vigil while his companions slept. He plotted their entry as best he could, not that things ever went totally according to plan; but some planning was better than none at all.

Just as the horizon swallowed the last rays of sunshine, Jack prodded the sleeping beauties from dreamland. He explained the plan and they set off.

After checking for any signs of Green's men, the trio approached the steel door. It was large, reinforced from the inside with a steel lock and no accessible hinges. Jack motioned for Rusty to climb up on his back and go for the second floor window. Rusty made the journey one foot over the other, kicking Jack in the shoulders and head several times along the way.

Jack struggled to push the shorter man high enough that he could reach the windowsill of the second floor.

Sonja stood guard, watching the street. She peered from left to right, monitoring every shadow or leaf that moved. It took only a few moments for her to grow agitated at the circus act behind her. She turned back toward the boys, walked up behind Jack and removed his kit from his back left pocket before ambling toward the door.

The door clicked, giving way on her first attempt. She pushed the door open and stepped inside. Her soft yet not-so-subtle cough caught the attention of the men still trying to mount the building.

Jack and Rusty looked at the door, at each other, back to the door, over to Sonja and finally back to each other. Rusty shrugged and leapt to the ground.

Sonja shined her fingers on her shirt smiling at the boys as they walked inside.

Jack felt around the wall to the right of the door for a light switch. A soft buzz grew louder as row after row of the lights came to life, illuminating the unending warehouse. The entire building was empty, except for row after row of tables with large light banks hanging over top of them. There was no way to tell what used to be on the tables, but Jack was sure they had been important at some point.

He couldn't see any dust, no cobwebs, no grease or oil. There was no dirt of any kind, yet the place looked deserted. It didn't make any sense and he wasn't about to wait around to figure it out. Jack moved toward a metal staircase, leading to a white paneled office stationed above the warehouse floor. He pointed at another staircase, leading up to the second floor on the opposite side of the warehouse, for Sonja and Rusty to investigate.

They went off in a rush, dodging in and out of stations along the way.

Jack began climbing the stairs. About halfway up he removed his hand from the railing and squeezed his fingers together. There was a distinct residue on his hand. He sniffed his fingers, detecting a strong smell of alcohol. Following a halfhearted lick of the end of his finger, Jack deduced some sort of cleaning solvent had been used on the staircase recently.

He arrived at the top of the stairs to find the painted white door there unlocked. The room was a 40 x 40 office, complete with an official desk, filing cabinets, a plastic plant and a well-worn leather couch. Jack searched behind the furniture in all the obvious places for anything resembling a safe. He found a few pens, balled up handkerchiefs and a few dust bunnies, but nothing requiring a combination.

Jack sat down at the desk to investigate the drawers, but a loud crash startled him back to his feet. It came from above and some distance away. He peered out over the warehouse floor without seeing any signs of disturbance.

Another crash echoed through the warehouse. Jack bolted out of the office, slid down the stairs and ran across the length of the warehouse. He flew up the other set of stairs to the third floor.

When he arrived, Sonja and Rusty were engaged in a brawl with Green's men, next to a large metal safe. Sonja had two thugs unconscious at her feet and was ducking and dodging a small man in a suit as he swung wildly. His left hook missed her jaw by a hair. She spun down, her left leg circling around the lower part of her body and the heel of her foot landing in the man's crotch. He crumpled over, falling to the ground in pain. Another man got hold of her around her waist, lifting her into the air.

Jack was mid stride when his fist landed on the assailant's kidney. The man shrieked in pain, releasing Sonja; she immediately came across to her left shoulder with a right hook, landing square in the thug's eye, air mailing him to dreamland.

They both turned their attention to the four men surrounding Rusty, who was using a broken post to fend them off. Each time one of them advanced, he would stab them or bash them in the leg or foot. Both Jack and Sonja came to his defense, Sonja taking a few running steps before leaping into a sliding kick, landing in the back of the knee of the furthest attacker. Her left arm pulled into the air, jutting forward across the man's face.

Jack grabbed an empty gun lying on the floor, half way between Rusty and the doorway. His left arm pitched sideways, sending the gun spinning at one man, nailing him on the side of the face and giving Rusty enough time to slam the post over his head. Jack tapped the closest man on the shoulder and presented him with his classic right hook.

Sonja and Rusty both turned to the last thug standing. His eyes bulged for the split-second he stood before taking off running. Rusty gave chase, but stopped at the staircase, waving his arm.

Jack pulled the small slip of paper out of his pocket and read the numbers to Sonja, who turned the safe dial with ease, having done it a million times at Star Lake. Rusty came up to them just as the door opened.

Inside the safe was a large yellow manila envelope, a small golden pin and a letter. Rusty grabbed for the pin and held it up to the light. The pin was small, only as big as a half dollar coin. It looked like a golden falcon with its wings spread wide. The light bounced off the polished edges.

"Well," Rusty declared with the pin between his teeth. "It's real gold. But seriously, a falcon? Could they be any less serious about the whole scary Syndicate thing?"

Sonja glared at Rusty. "Vince had one just like it."

Jack shook his head and then proceeded to read the letter out loud.

To All Bosses,
We have grown tired of your inability to work together. As of this notice, only one man can be the town boss. Whoever brings the falcon to us at the docks by noon on the 25th will rule this town. The others will be dealt with. Use any means necessary.
Do not disappoint us.

"This is from the Syndicate. The war between the bosses must've gotten out of control to the point they no longer wanted to deal with the mess." Jack stated the obvious.

"Yeah. And Green is not going to be happy we took his little bird," said Rusty.

"On the contrary," announced Mr. Green. "I couldn't have done this without you."

Jack, Sonja and Rusty spun around at the same time to see Green, Damon, and a dozen well-armed suits standing directly behind them.

CHAPTER TWENTY FOUR

"It's nothing personal," said Green, as his men surrounded the trio. "You have been excellent pawns. I might never have gained control without your impeccable, unwitting assistance. You see, when Damon killed Vincent, the pin should have been mine. But our dearly departed friend, Winters, locked away Damon's trophy, refusing to divulge its location. We thought it a lost cause until you led us right to our prize."

He laughed with Damon. "Oh, I love how shortsighted most people can be. They never even realize the traps they walk right into..."

"Until it's too late," Damon chimed in.

Sonja giggled, drawing Damon's attention. "What exactly are you giggling about, woman?"

"It's funny how smart you think you are," she continued giggling.

"Sonja," cautioned Rusty. "Please try not to aggravate the dozen large men pointing guns at us."

"I'm sorry. It's just funny that they think they're the only ones who can set a trap."

A crash thundered from the floor below. Green's men watched in horror as an enormous truck came barreling through the front door, half way into the warehouse. Dozens of heavily armed police poured in from the hole it left in the wall.

The passenger side door of the truck opened as a man hopped out, using it for cover.

"You're surrounded, Green. Why don't you be a good boy and put down your weapons," yelled Commissioner Davis at the top of his lungs.

"You three, deal with them. The rest of you get to the rails," barked Green. His men took positions along the railing pointing their guns downward at the open warehouse floor.

"Fire," screamed Green in response.

Bullets burrowed their way to the steel of the building, chipping brick and chopping wood along the way. The firefight between the two forces raged on as Damon and his three goons advanced.

Rusty charged forward like a bull, catapulting himself into the mid-section of the goon the furthest on the right. He fell backward with the weight of Rusty on his chest, knocking into Green who fell backward, half way down the stairs, with his replacement emerald cane still clutched in his hand.

Damon pointed at the two remaining thugs and then at Jack. His focus stayed on Sonja, who took a few steps back away from the railing, so as not to get hit by a stray bullet.

Jack let the two men circle him, keeping his guard up and legs moving. He dodged a few incoming punches before taking a kick to the back, sending him crumpled to the floor. One man picked up Jack, locking his arms behind him, exposing his torso to the other attacker. He took a left and then a right to the solar plexus.

"Jack," Sonja cried out.

"Why don't you worry about yourself, right now, doll," winked Damon, pulling out his serrated blade.

She took his advice and refocused on the task at hand. Sonja stopped backpedaling. Her stance changed, placing one foot in front of the other, spread far apart front to back. She raised her right arm, extended her hand and middle finger.

Damon laughed. "You're gonna get it." He swayed back and forth in an attempt to confuse her on his approach. She tossed a left hook that landed in his stomach staggering him for only a second. She swept with her right leg, rounding her body, connecting with the back of his legs.

His head cracked off the ground, sending pulses of pain down his back as if electricity had shot down his spine.

Sonja looked over at Rusty, seeing him scuffling with a man by the stairs. She looked to her left and noted Jack had thrown off the man holding his arms, but was taking punches faster than he was giving them.

"I told you to pay attention," Damon said as he rolled up on his left side, grabbing her around the ankles and toppling Sonja to the ground. She threw her arms out in front of her to stop the momentum, injuring her right wrist and yelping in pain.

Damon proceeded to climb on top of her, straddling his hips over the top of hers. He pulled the knife up between their faces, twisting it side to side, the light bouncing off the vicious blade in various directions. He pinned her left arm down, allowing her right arm to remain free when he saw the bone sticking out of her wrist. The smell of grease and a lack of showering assaulted Sonja's nose. His breath made the air around her taste like garbage.

He leaned down and licked her face. "Pity we don't have more time." He raised his arm up with the knife. A sneer was plastered on his face, eyes locked her cleavage, drooling over his prey.

"Sonja," roared Jack, catching a glimpse of her with Damon on top of her, raising his knife in the air. Damon glanced over at him and waved as one of the goons landed a kick to Jack's chest while he was distracted.

Rusty heard Jack yell. His eyes found Sonja pinned under the massive thug. He punched his attacker with two rights in a frenzy and flopped over, grasping for the nearest heavy object he could find before launching it in Sonja's direction.

The emerald cane pinged off the side of Damon's head before dropping with a clank on the floor beside them. Damon was dazed and in a panic he plunged the knife down, slicing the top of Sonja's left shoulder and burying the blade into the wooden paneling covering the cement floor. Despite the pain in her shoulder, she kicked out his legs, nailing him as hard as she could in the balls.

He fell over, grimacing. Sonja followed through, rolling over on top of Damon, squeezing his thighs together with her hips putting more pressure on the injury. She reached over with her good arm, plucking his shiny toy from its wooden imprisonment.

She winked at him. He looked up to see the blade shining like a star.

"Pay attention," she thundered, bringing the blade down to its new home, six inches deep in his heart.

She rolled off Damon's soon-to-be corpse and onto her back, where she caught her breath.

Sonja staggered to her feet before falling back to her knees. Jack tossed one of the attackers over the edge of the railing and Rusty had engaged the other long enough to allow Jack to grab the man by the collar of his shirt, throwing them into one of the gunmen firing on the crew below, sending both plummeting to their deaths.

The smell of burning cherry wood filled Jack's mouth with an awful burned barbecue taste. Smoke was beginning to cloud the air around them as fire raged below, ignited by hot bullets ricocheting off cement and wood.

The fire had fully engulfed the white office on the second level, overlooking the main floor.

Jack stumbled over to Sonja, reaching down to help her up off of the ground. Rusty rushed to their side to bolster Sonja with Jack like bookends. The ceiling was crackling above them. Embers flew and debris was beginning to fall from the rafters.

As the trio headed for the stairs, the shaking hand of Mr. Green rose from the ground, grabbed the wall and he dragged himself to his feet. He stood and walked forward, pushing them back away from the exit.

Jack released himself from Sonja, putting her weight on Rusty. He stepped away from them, leading Green back away from the stairwell, deeper into the room. Rusty maneuvered Sonja over to the stairs and then dropped out from holding her up by leaning her against a wall.

Just as Rusty stepped forward to engage Green with Jack, a large piece of rafter infested with flames landed on the ground behind Green effectively blocking Rusty out and the two of them in.

Blood dripped from the corner of Jack's mouth. He held his left arm against his rib cage from the earlier matches and circled Green, dancing back and forth. Green's chest swelled with anger, puffing outward and releasing a booming yell. He hurled himself at Jack, sending them both crashing to the ground.

Jack and Green exchanged blows, hitting each other in the stomach, jaw and head. They rolled over each other to the left, getting in what shots they could; then to the right, swapping more rounds.

Green slammed his clenched fist in to Jack's rib cage, bringing tears to Jack's eyes, his body dropping limp to the ground. He climbed up the safe to stand above the Finder.

Reeling in pain, thrashing and turning while holding his chest, Jack had only a few seconds before Green continued his assault. Green pulled back his left leg, taking aim at the bloodied spots on his opponent's shirt. Jack desperately tried to use his arms to protect his broken ribs.

One kick after another came until Green finally missed, giving Jack the opportunity to roll away, butting right up against Damon's corpse.

"I always come out on top, Mr. Finder. You should've worked with me. We could have been kings," boasted Green as he raised his right leg over Jack's head.

Jack felt the debris-laden floor around him. His fingers felt metal just within his grasp. He clawed for it, reaching out for his life. With one final lurch, his forefingers latched onto the object, willing it closer.

Jack clutched the headpiece of Green's cane in his hand. He swung it over his body, unsheathing the razor thin blade and plunged it upward, lancing Mr. Green's torso with a primal scream.

A white hue washed over the green-suited man as he scrambled backwards away from Jack. He looked down at the headpiece and back up at Jack.

Green fell to the ground, against the rail, holding his stomach.

Jack grabbed the metal case, using it as a crutch to get on his feet. He limped over to Green, fire raging and all of Green's gang dead around them.

"This was your choice," uttered Jack, as he reached down pulling out the emerald blade, returning it to its home and handing the cane to its rightful owner.

The ceiling above cracked, raining down more debris. Jack looked to the exit. The stairway was painted in flame. He looked back to the railing. It was littered with the dead bodies of Green's men, but the steel railing was not aflame.

He ran over to the edge to see Sonja and Rusty being ushered out through the hole in the wall. Jack backed away from the railing and looked up towards the windows above.

The ceiling crackled again, louder. A visible crack down the middle of the roof held a raging flaming chasm. He looked at the railing again, took a deep breath and, with a running start, leapt over the banister.

CHAPTER TWENTY FIVE

"Jack? Can you hear me? Jack?"

The bells of a high-pitched whine rang out in excruciating decibels in Jack's ears. He blinked rapidly. Too blurred figures stood to his left and one larger one to his right.

"Jack. You're in the hospital, but you're okay. Can you hear me?"

Jack nodded

He closed his eyes as tight as he could and concentrated on focusing. He turned his head to the right and then opened his eyes. As everything came in the focus, he recognized the smooth skinned face above him.

"Hey," he took a long pause. "What's up, lady doc?"

He felt a sudden pain hit the top of his head.

"Ouch," he exclaimed turning his head to the left to see Rusty giggling, looking up at Sonja. Her eyes fixed on him with her arm raised to hit him again.

"Behave, you two, he's not a well man."

"I could've told you that before this all started," said a voice from the bottom of Jack's bed.

Jack pushed himself up in his hospital bed. He put his hands to his eyes, rubbing them with his fists to push out the blur. He looked down at the other end to see a small blond haired man, in a matching hospital gown, leaning on the bottom of his bed.

"Caleb," Jack exclaimed then coughed.

"I told you he was too stubborn to die," toted Rusty. Caleb raised his crutch and slapped Rusty upside the head. Sonja followed suit, slapping him again.

"Bunch of no sense of humor having--" Rusty trailed off, muttering to himself.

"You had seven broken ribs, a punctured lung and a concussion, but we've patched you up. You're going to be just fine," smiled the attractive doctor.

"My head really hurts," complained Jack.

"Yeah. It's going to, for a few days."

"Where is your adoring husband? Shouldn't he be here, rooting for the coma?"

"No. He said he had something to take care of today."

Jack nodded.

"You know, I always wanted to date a doctor," Rusty, announced stroking his beard.

"And I always wanted to be a fairy princess," said the doctor as she smiled, waved and moseyed out of the room.

Rusty frowned. Caleb chortled.

Jack looked around for a minute as his three amigos carried on. The room was illuminated by the early morning sun. The equipment above him beeped and bopped in rhythm with his heart. He was grateful to be alive and even happier to be surrounded by his companions, but something still felt off. He thought it might just have been the awful cotton taste in his mouth.

The beats increased in frequency.

"What is today's date?" asked Jack.

Sonja answered "the 25th – why?"

He looked at her and then Rusty.

"You're not thinking," Sonja was interrupted by Jack yanking the IV, monitors and electrodes from his body. He hopped up, out of his bed, and grabbed the clothes off the chair next to his bed. Jack put his pants on under his gown, ripped it off and threw on his shirt.

"Jack, c'mon, you need rest," sounded his companions.

"I will. But I need to see this through, first," he answered, wincing.

"Sonja. Rusty. Let's go," Jack called behind him as he rushed out of the hospital room.

CHAPTER TWENTY SIX

The gentle rocking of the waves made the boats lining either side of the dock seem to dance before them. Jack loved the unmistakable smell of open water. Big body, small body, it didn't matter. He enjoyed being on any kind of liquid freedom.

Off at the end of the dock stood the largest vessel Jack had ever seen. It stretched well beyond the length of the dock, with a covered top deck, shielded by glass on all sides; the boat could easily hold a hundred people. The jet black paint gave it the illusion of being smaller than it really was. In white lettering, the name 'Natasha'' stood out as the only distinguishable marking on the entire package.

The only indication of the true size of the ship was the comparison against two six foot tall bruisers that stood on either side of the dock. They held massive guns, pointed in the air, their fingers caressing the triggers. Their eyes were hidden behind the black shielding of their sunglasses, but as Jack and company approached the boat, the guns lowered in their direction.

Sonja and Jack put their hands in the air, nudging Rusty to do the same. They approached with caution, stepping slowly without any sudden movement. On the front of the ship, a mounted belt-fed cannon pointing out over the ocean. Next to it stood an angry looking fellow gripping the weapon as if it were a life raft and he was lost at sea.

Impressive looking guard number one patted them down, one at a time, as they stood against the boat. Guard number two kept watch, in case they tried anything funny. Although, the last thing any of them, even the wisecracking Rusty, felt like doing was making a joke with that kind of volatile firepower nearby.

Once satisfied with their status as non-hostile, one of the guards escorted the group onto the ship and into its bowls. The hardwood creaked under their feet as they walked forward. Jack noted no driver at the helm, meaning they weren't in a hurry to leave. The rooms below deck were larger than Jack had figured a yacht could carry.

As one door sealed behind them, the guard turned to the side of a black door. The entire interior of the ship was covered in dark colors. Light beamed on the path by circular lights lined up overhead, leading directly to the door. The guard opened the door, revealing a panel of three chairs sitting behind a large desk, situated underneath the rear of the boat. There were plaques and weapons hanging on the wall behind the chairs. It was difficult to see in such a dark environment, but Jack felt as if the seats were not empty.

The group was ushered forward at the insistence of the guerrilla behind them. They piled up just outside of a large bright light, shining from the ceiling pointing down on a man kneeling in front of the ominous panel.

"I swear I don't know about any bird," pleaded a familiar voice.

Jack took one step to his right, getting an angle on the man sweating underneath the hot light. Commissioner Davis laid himself on his knees and palms, staring at the ground. He wore civilian clothing, a blue pair of jeans with a drenched plaid shirt that was ripped around the sleeves. Jack had never seen Davis in this type of position before, but he would recognize his voice anywhere.

"I came here as the letter said, to claim my rightful place as the one true boss of this town," he stated as fact. "You owe me, after everything I have done."

"Silence," boomed a deep voice, emanating from the shadows. It echoed across the room and back again, beating their ears.

"We owe you nothing. You are the one who let things get out of control in the first place. If it wasn't for you, we would not be here at all."

Jack expected bolts of lightning to start striking the ground at any moment, following the thunderous voice echoing from everywhere around them.

Davis fell back down, touching his forehead to the ground, shivering from head to toe. "Yes, master," he forced out through his closed throat.

"We have your falcon," Jack announced, pushing off on his heels to seem as tall as possible. He reached behind his back, flapping his hand open and closed. Rusty reached deep into his pocket, pulling out a golden pin in the shape of a falcon. It was heavy and glimmered in the light.

Jack's left hand thrust the pin up into the air. The pin shone as Jack pointed the falcon toward the nothingness in front of them.

A small man appeared from the shadows, five feet in front of them. He stepped forward, one foot in front of the other, with the large gaping movements of an honor guard. The man extended his arms, holding his hands cupped out in front of his body. Jack lowered the falcon toward the white gloves, pausing long enough to receive a slight nod from the gentleman, confirming the action. Once in possession of the pin, the man stepped backward, disappearing into the shadows from which he came.

"Excellent," hissed a raspy voice. "It has been decided."

"What? No," exclaimed Davis, rising to his feet. "You can't be serious."

"What has been decided? What are you talking about?" Jack raised his eyebrows. His eyes had the same look as someone who had just been shot, without all the screaming. He raised his arm like a school-boy, eagerly awaiting the teacher to call on him.

Then the lights dimmed.

The door behind them opened, flooding the room with a bright white light. Jack placed his hand above his eyes, squinting. He took a few steps forward, leading the group out of the basement dwelling. Every light on the boat had been turned on around them, making the ordinary black interior bounce beams of light off the walls and into their line of sight.

When they climbed back up the small staircase to the top deck, the guards had stationed themselves on the boat, minus the one waiting for them to the step off the boat.

"Sir," said the one who had frisked them, just moments before, bowing before Jack and extending one arm to point the way out.

Rusty escorted the visibly shaken Davis along the path. The two walked over to the edge of the dock, sitting down and staring out onto the open water. They whispered to each other and shook their heads.

Jack pulled Sonja's hand, tugging her off the ship as her head craned about absorbing every detail. Just after Jack's foot left the thin metal of the step off the boat, the soft purr coming from the engine escalated into a tremendous hum. The boat began pulling away at a high rate of speed. Within seconds there was nothing but ripples of disturbed water left in its wake. Just like that, it was gone.

Sonja stood, blinking in disbelief. She was impressed by how fast such a large ship became a blur on the horizon. Her gaze turned to the two men sitting on the edge of the dock.

"Guys," she called out, motioning for them to approach. She stood by Jack's side, locked her hand in his, intertwining their fingers and squeezing them together. Sonja took a deep breath.

"Anyone want to tell me what just happened there?"

Davis looked white as a ghost. "Do you know

how much I've gone through, only to have you steal everything from me? I won't forget this, Finder." He tore off his tattered shirt and threw it to the ground in front of Jack before storming away.

Jack looked at Rusty with a halfhearted smile. "I didn't want it to turn out like this."

"Not to worry," Rusty said, turning to watch Davis kick every item in his path back to the parking lot. "I'm definitely not the one you need to be worried about."

"Besides, I've come to like calling you Boss, anyway." Rusty said with a grin. "Let's go break my brother out of the place making him wear a dress and grab a pint. Yeah?"

He started down the dock, leaving Jack and Sonja standing on the edge of the water alone together.

Jack stared out onto the open water over Sonja's head. He pulled her to him with a firm yet gentle grip. She melted into his arms, burying her head against his chest. His hand danced up her back and cradled her head as they enjoyed the moment, embracing each other's warmth.

"What happens now?" she asked, looking up into his eyes.

He smiled back without uttering a word and lowered his head, gently pressing his lips against hers. Their tender moment lasted only a few seconds, but to Jack it felt like a lifetime of waiting was finally over.

He broke the seal between them, moving his head upward to kiss her forehead gently. "Come on.

We have a town to run."

Jack Breeder will return

Be the first to hear about Jack's upcoming adventures!

Sign Up Now

Your email address will never be shared and you can unsubscribe at any time.

Acknowledgements

Dear reader,

First and foremost, let me say THANK YOU for reading.

I have to thank my editors. You are amazing. Without your help this book may never have come to life. Thank you for everything you did to make this book a success.

Dean Wesley Smith and Kristine Kathryn Rusch, for being my writing mentors, thank you for everything you taught me. But thank you most of all for teaching me to write for myself and not for you. You helped fill my toolbox and then sent me on my way. Thank you for believing in me.

Thank you to my first readers, even those who didn't have time to finish reading before publication, thank you for your support.

And finally thank you to my mom, brothers and sisters from other mothers, friends, and acquaintances. I truly believe that who we are is the sum of all of our experiences. Without any of you I would not be who I am today. Thank you for being characters in my story.

Dedication:

"You don't always get to pick what you do in life."

-Anonymous

I have found this to be one of the most honest and frightening truths in life. We don't choose the body and mind we're born into. We don't always get to choose what we''re going to do, but it is in those specific actions, those things we choose to do <u>willingly</u> that define who we are.

Life simply gives you the *sand*; it's up to you to build the *castle*.

This book is dedicated to Marsha Spohn and Mark Barlet. You gave me the strength and courage to find out who I am by the choices I made, and not those that life made for me. For that, I will always be grateful.

About Steven Rome

Award-winning author Steven Spohn turns once again to fiction under the name in his newest novel *The Finder*. Featured on CNN, NBC and other mainstream news outlets as a technology expert, Steven brings all his knowledge and much more to his gripping new novel.

As editor-in-chief of , Steven manages the world's largest charity dedicated to improving the lives of children, adults and veterans with disabilities. Under his leadership, AbleGamers continually receives critical acclaim for excellence in communications from today's top leaders including the mayor of New York City.

In his spare time, Steven writes for many national publications and international journals. Steven currently resides in his hometown of Pittsburgh, Pennsylvania.